D1490589

FOR THE LOVE OF LAURALEE

A For the Love Of
Historical Romance

Other books by CJ Love:

A Horse Called Hustle
Ring Around His Heart

The For the Love Of Historical Romance Series
For the Love of Murphy

FOR THE LOVE OF LAURALEE

•

CJ Love

AVALON BOOKS

NEW YORK

Published by Avalon Books,
an imprint of Thomas Bouregy & Co., Inc.
160 Madison Avenue, New York, NY 10016

Library of Congress Cataloging-in-Publication Data

Love, CJ.
    For the love of Lauralee / CJ Love.
        p.   cm.
    ISBN 978-0-8034-7661-5 (acid-free paper)
    I. Title.
    PS3612.O83385F66 2011
    813'.6–dc22

                        2010046200

PRINTED IN THE UNITED STATES OF AMERICA
ON ACID-FREE PAPER
BY RR DONNELLEY, BLOOMSBURG, PENNSYLVANIA

*This story is dedicated to my sister,
Carol Cherry, along with precious memories
of her daughter Lauralee.*

Chapter One

June 1902

The gypsies had returned. Dante didn't know if the township of Omaha had given them permission to erect vendor booths along the road or if the Roma people did it on their own accord. Whichever the case, they arrived once a year, and when night fell, university students from Creighton roved between the booths buying baubles and charms and paying fifty cents to have their palms read.

Strands of bulb lights crisscrossed above the booths and the cobblestone roadway. A fellow wearing a wide-brimmed hat and spangled vest played the accordion as he glided through the multitude. Dante moved along too, not to buy trinkets, but to return to his dorm room. He didn't like crowds, and he didn't like gypsies.

A woman stepped off the curb, surprising him. *"T'aves mansa."* She had the allure of a minx, with raven curls and flashing eyes. Large hoops dangled from her earlobes.

"What did you say?"

"T'aves mansa. Come with me." Her tone was as provocative as the neckline of her crimson blouse.

1

A beauty she may have been, but Dante didn't trust her, and he stepped wide to move along. "I'm on my way home. Excuse me."

Someone caught his arm. "I saw you trying to sneak back to your boring law books, and I won't allow it." Lamont Humphrey stood taller than Dante and had a thin boyish build, and in the bulb lights his hair looked like strands of hay. "There's a monkey playing poker with Clarence and Robert across the road. Come on." He caught sight of the Roma woman. "Oh. Hellooo."

She didn't look at him. Instead, with fiery eyes, black as ink, she asked Dante, "What *natsia* do you belong, eh?"

"I don't belong to anything." It annoyed him that she was pursuing the conversation. She was acting as if she knew him, or *should* know him, as if they had a history of some sort. Because he had black hair and eyes like hers didn't mean he was related to her in any way.

Several people passed behind him. A man laughed, and a young woman squealed in return. Their jostling pushed Dante closer to the gypsy, and he grew more rigid. She frowned at him. "Who are you?"

"My name is Quinn." He knew he sounded like an oldster with a cane who was tired of the lights and the noise, but he wanted her to leave him alone.

She furrowed her brow. "Quinn? That is not a Roma name."

"He's not gypsy," Lamont told her, and he slapped Dante on the shoulder. "He's a law student, magna cum laude, with a job waiting for him in San Francisco."

Mystified, she scrutinized him further. "You are *gaje?*"

"*Gaje,*" Lamont mimicked. He glanced between Dante and the gypsy. "That's a serious-sounding word, isn't it? What does it mean?"

"It is a name for those who are not Roma." Sudden as a lashing cat, she captured Dante's hand and searched his face with her velvet eyes. "*Va.* Your blood is as cold as night rain. You're a thorny bush, *va?* The Roma, our blood is hot. Hot with magic."

Dante snatched his hand from hers, disturbed by the heat of her skin.

"She has you nailed," Lamont cut in, gripping Dante's shoulder. "Cold and thorny, that's you. Never have any fun. Always in control of your emotions and highly disciplined." He grinned at the black-eyed woman. "Now, what's this about magic? Will you read my fortune?" He released Dante's shoulder and folded the woman's arm into his. "I've just graduated, and I have no idea which job offer to take."

"Come, we will consult the sphere," she told him softly, ignoring Dante.

Lamont winked at him. "I'm off to consult the sphere. Go home to your law books, and, eh, don't wait up for me."

Watching Lamont cross the road with the gypsy, Dante let out his breath and unclenched his jaw. No one had ever guessed that he was Roma before, and of course he was not wholly so, but only half Roma.

It shamed him to be gypsy. Vagabonds were what people called them, outlaws and thieves and drifters. He would not be counted among them. He'd earned his law degree. He'd taken an oath, and he meant to abide by it. No one would ever know his family background if Dante could help it.

Stepping toward the wrought-iron gates of the school, Dante paused when two men darted in front of him and ran ahead. Their voices melded with the crowd's noise. He watched them a moment, and then something caught his eye. Gems fixed on twine spiraled in a booth window. In the low lights they sparkled like varied stars. He concentrated on the red jewel, for it

reminded him of something. It was a fragment of a recollec-
tion, an old one too, one that pulled him back to a more innocent
time. He was home on Nob Hill. A woman sang in the parlor . . .
Dante stepped closer, trying to place the memory.

"Why such anger when Roza asked if you are Roma?"

Dante gazed beyond the gem and into the booth lit with tiny
candles. He saw a woman's outline but not her face.

"It is good to be gypsy, *va?*" Her voice sounded aged and
heavily accented. "You have strong nose like my father. He was
from the *Lowara natsia*. Skilled with horses, my father, very
fine, and you, *Chikno,* do you like the horses?"

He had no idea what *Chikno* meant, but he latched on to the
other word he'd heard before. "*Natsia?* What does *natsia*
mean?"

She stepped forward and the light hit her round face. Deep
lines cut across her forehead. She wore many chains around
her wrinkled neck and a kerchief over her long silver hair.

When he saw her eyes, Dante remembered her, and he caught
his breath.

"*Natsia,*" she explained without noticing his reaction. "Clan,
you would say. There are many clans in one *natsia*. My father
was *Lowara* and my mother *Kalderasha.*" She touched the bottom of the gems with her fingers. The red one twirled. "I am my
mother's daughter, *Kalderasha*. We are old and remember the
old ways, the spells, the curses, and the enchantments." She
raised the curtain on the side of the booth. "Come. We will
see your past and your future."

Stiffened with hostility, Dante stepped into the small cubicle.
It smelled strangely sweet and mysterious. Cloves, he thought,
and ginger.

"Sit," she told him, pointing to a stool and table. The booth was barely large enough for the two of them. He sat and watched her pull a tiny cup from her skirt pocket. Spitting into it, she said, "You are Roma. I feel it." She took a pinch of dry leaves and rubbed them between her fingers. "It is your bloodline that we will decide. We will read the leaves."

"I abhor my bloodline," Dante said, seething. "I am revolted by my heritage."

"Roza was wrong. You are not cold, as she said. There is passion inside of you, much *chingary,* but you must learn to possess it if you will get what you crave. What is it that you desire?"

"Desire?" Bitterness welled in his chest. The edges of his mouth pressed downward so firmly that he had trouble saying, "I suppose it's revenge—Emelina."

She didn't look surprised; her features barely changed. Then she opened her mouth and let out an earsplitting scream.

Startled, Dante fell partway off the stool and backward against the wall. The booth shifted. A weak board caved against his arm, and he shoved at the thin partition. With a loud clap, the board fell onto the cobblestones. Dante staggered sideways as the remaining walls fell and the cloth roof floated onto the road. People stared silently. Someone laughed. Another applauded.

In his peripheral vision he saw movement. Long silver hair swayed and disappeared into the crowd. Dante ran forward, wedging himself into the throng. Lamont called Dante's name, but he ran regardless, colliding with the shoulders and backs of those ambling along. He stopped near the archway and fountain, inhaling deeply and looking in all directions for her.

There.

Dante lurched again, propelling himself forward, tossing everything in his path out of his way. He hopped over a basket of hats and skidded right.

Blackness swelled in the narrow passageway. He stopped, breathless, and took a step forward. The crowd's noise and music faded. Stench replaced the sticky-sweet smell on the street. He crouched, hearing a footstep. Fingers strummed a chord on a guitar directly behind him, and Dante spun around.

And then they were upon him. Fists caught him in his ribs and kidneys. An arm came around his neck, dragging him backward.

Dante knew how to fight. He'd boxed on the college team, and he replied with good punches before knuckles smashed his jaw. When he fell to the cobblestones, boots kicked him in his side. In the dim light he saw that there were three men hovering over him. Pressing his arms to his side, Dante tried to lessen the injury to his ribs. They continued to beat him and kick him. At last, one of the men knelt beside him and grabbed his hair.

Shrouded in half-light from the street, Emelina bent before him. She uttered, *"Amaria."* Louder: *"Gajengi baxt. Tooti tshor . . . chor, Butji, amaria!"*

The man holding his hair laughed. *"Amaria.* The *Kalderasha* curses you. You carry the gypsy curse. You will become the one that you despise: a thief and a drifter."

It was Lamont who found him bleeding in the alley and helped him to a clinic. There, a doctor cleaned Dante's wounds and covered him in bandages. For a day and a half he remained in bed. Saturday evening he sat in his dorm room and stared into the night. Beyond the opened window he could see the street. The gypsies had gone. Emelina had gone.

Shame caused him to slump farther onto the window seat. He'd chased her through the streets like a madman. He, Dante Quinn, reasonable, self-restrained man that he was, had behaved like a lunatic. He'd deserved a beating.

He'd scared her when he'd said he wanted revenge. In her panic, Emelina had sought protection. In fear, she'd cursed Dante to scare him off. It wouldn't work. He would find her again—but carefully next time.

If he was anything, he was intentional, not passionate as she'd claimed. Studying law had taught him shrewdness and discretion. He was purposely dispassionate. Deliberately deliberate. He glanced around the dorm room, the beige and brown of it all. Everything had its place: chair tucked in beneath the desk, books stacked neatly, ink bottle capped—perfect.

Dante shifted his weight on the window seat, panting from the sore muscles around his ribs and taking a deeper breath before the knifing pain took it away. His back hurt too, and his left leg. Usually, he won his boxing matches at the club, so he wasn't used to aches and pains afterward. And mostly, Dante fought one person at a time, not three, so he supposed it would take him another day or two to regain his comfort. Relaxing back, he stared out the window again. The sky was clear, and the sinking moon was shining brightly. Movement captured his attention. Something, someone, crossed the lawn. And then Dante saw a woman by the gate. Her long silver hair lifted with the breeze.

With a start, he pushed to his feet. Was it Emelina who was watching his window? Did she want to speak to him, as he wanted to speak to her? His injuries kept him from racing downstairs, so he raised his hand to motion to her . . .

She moved backward, and darkness shrouded her figure as if she were only an apparition ebbing into the shadows. Dante hit the wall with his good fist. Why had she come, if not to speak to him? It didn't matter, he thought, quickly managing his temper. He would find Emelina again, he would search the

entire state of Nebraska—and Kansas too, if he must. The
Ticktin Law Group expected him in three weeks, and the ticket
Dante bought was meant for the following Thursday. He supposed he could return the ticket, exchange it for another. Perhaps he could rent a room and borrow Lamont's automobile to
search the surrounding areas of town. Gypsies traveled from
place to place. Surely their caravan would be easy to find.
With his mind set, he limped toward the bed and pulled out
the travel case beneath it.

A tapping noise woke him. Another round of knocking
sounded at the door. Dante got out of bed, and while moving
through the front room, he stubbed his toe on the traveling trunk
he'd put out the previous night. Scowling, he opened the
door.

A policeman stood there. His blue uniform was buttoned to
his neck, and he wore a good-conduct chevron on his sleeve.
Removing his hat, the man said, "Good morning, sir."

Dante continued to frown at him and glanced into the quiet
hallway. Several students moved about; most still wore their
pajamas and robes. They didn't try to disguise their curiosity
as they stared at the officer.

"Two of your classmates are missing items from their dorm
rooms." The policeman glimpsed at the notepad in his hand.
"A money clip and a pair of cuff links." Looking up, he said,
"I wonder if you have anything missing as well."

" 'Missing'? There's been a burglary?"

The officer considered Dante's bandaged hand. "Two rooms
have been burgled, yes. I'd like you to check your rooms to see
if you're missing anything." His eyes darted into the room.
"When I was outside, I noticed that your window is open."

Dante twisted around to see the glass. Hadn't he closed it

last night? It accounted for the fresh morning air that drifted through the curtains and the cool wood floor beneath his bare feet.

"Would you have a look around, sir?"

"Of course," Dante said, stepping backward into the room and leaving the door opened.

Nothing looked out of place. He returned to his bedroom and gazed at the blankets and mattress, the closed window, and the desk still piled high with books.

A beam of sunlight caught a sparkle on top of the dresser. Dante stepped forward and lifted the jewelry off the wood. Cuff links. Bills folded over and fastened together with a clip. These weren't his. Where had they come from?

You will become the one that you despise: a thief and a drifter.

A throb of panic pounded through him as if it vibrated through the whole dorm building. Good God.

Opening the top drawer of the dresser, he scraped the items inside and shut it noisily.

"Sir?"

Dante returned to the door. "Sorry," he told the officer. "I was just having a close look. Nothing's missing here." He swallowed hard at the acrid taste in his mouth.

The man stared curiously. "Are you certain?"

"Yes, I . . . I'm positive," Dante told him, knowing he sounded nervous. He cleared his throat and held on to the door-knob in an attempt at casualness.

"What's happened to you? Why are you bandaged?"

Dante glanced at his left hand and the three-day-old bandage that was half-unwrapped from sleeping on it. "Er . . . fight," he told the officer. "I'm a boxer."

"May I come inside?"

"Why?" Acquainted with the law as he was, Dante knew the officer couldn't have a search warrant on him already. "I told you nothing is missing."

"Running off somewhere?"

"Excuse me?"

The officer nodded toward the travel trunk near the table, the one Dante had tripped over getting to the door.

Facing the officer squarely, he attempted a confident tone. "Is there anything else?"

"No," the officer told him and returned the hat to his head. "But don't run off"—he checked his notepad again—"Mr. Quinn."

Dante shut the door firmly as alarm swept through his veins. Limping to the bedroom again, he jerked open the dresser drawer. The cuff links and money clip slid forward. His hand shook as he reached for them.

How did they get here?

He'd gone to bed with the last of his pain medication that the doctor had given him. He hadn't slept well at first, and he'd dreamed of Nob Hill.

Maybe he'd had a bad reaction to the medicine. Had he walked in his sleep and taken articles from his neighbors? Could he have gone through windows, balanced on the ledge, and lifted jewelry pieces off bureaus and dressers while sleep-walking?

Outrageous.

Dante's mind strained for facts. *Zachary Wheeler vs. County of Princeton*, 1803. Wheeler had been accused of chicken thievery, and he had used sleepwalking as his defense. The court found him innocent by rule of doubt after three jury members spent the night watching Wheeler's bedroom. The old man had apparently scrambled out his window, walked to the neighbor's pen, and began to pluck a chicken—alive.

Ipso facto: By the fact itself. Innocent.

Ipso facto: The jewelry lay in Dante's drawer. Guilty.

Chapter Two

Should he ask Lamont if the cuff links belonged to him? They'd been roommates for five years, and on occasion both of them had ended up with each other's belongings.

No, no good. If the cuff links didn't belong to Lamont, then Lamont would know that Dante was in possession of stolen property. As good-natured as Lamont Humphrey was, he would never turn a blind eye to thievery. It was best to leave Lamont out of it.

But what was the alternative? Turn himself in to the police? Dante's chest tightened at the thought. His career, just starting, would be mashed like a cigar in a tray. Stamped ashes smoldering to nothingness.

Did he carry the *Kalderasha* curse?

Dante slammed the drawer shut. He refused to believe a gypsy had cursed him. No one could cause another person to do something against his will simply by chanting mumbo jumbo above their heads.

Outrageous. Superstitious hocus-pocus.

He opened the drawer again. Emelina had cursed him with

the *suggestion.* That's what she'd done. She'd suggested that he steal and then, in his drugged state . . .

Dante pulled the jewelry from the drawer. He would drop it somewhere, somewhere his dormmates would find it: outside, maybe, or in the hall when no one watched him. Then he would begin his search for Emelina. He put the jewelry into his pocket and walked out of the bedroom.

He'd never driven so fast. It thrilled him, in a strange way. He supposed it was because he'd spent the better part of five years in a classroom and in a dorm room writing papers. He glanced at the speedometer. Fourteen miles per hour!

Dante hadn't driven much, except for the last several days. He'd searched the countryside for Emelina's caravan. At last, yesterday, he'd followed her into Forge Rock. Emelina had seen him; that was why she'd ran; that was why she'd boarded the train.

He tightened his hands on the steering wheel and pressed his foot hard on the accelerator. There was no roof on the car, and the air whipped his hair like a flag in a windstorm. Driving was a bit like riding a horse, he decided. The automobile jumped and quivered like a kicking mustang. Trees passed in a rush. The rutted trail wound toward the railroad tracks and then took measure beside them. He saw the train again, the caboose of it anyway. Puffs of smoke exhaled into the blue sky.

By God, he was catching up!

With his index finger, Dante wiped at his goggles, trying to see clearly. Someone stood outside one of the passenger cars, on the platform of it. It was a worker . . . No! It was a woman in a skirt and billowing blouse. Her gray hair floated with the wind, tunneling through the spaces between rail cars. She held a red scarf in her hand. It appeared as if she spoke to someone, but no one stood with her. As Dante drove closer, he saw that Emelina's eyes were closed. Her lips moved. And then she released the scarf. It drifted on the breeze, spiraled and twisted, and then settled on the Packard's windshield. A fringed edge caught the lip of the metal surrounding the glass and the fabric fluttered in Dante's face.

He stamped the brakes with both feet. The back end of the car shimmied violently, and the scarf blew upward and off the glass.

Now he could see, and suddenly he wished he couldn't. The back of the car, still sliding, skated toward the trunk of an elm tree. Dante gunned the engine. Rear tires spun crazily, then caught, and the Packard flew forward again.

But not on the trail. Steering this way, that way, and trying to avoid the trunk of an old oak, he roared over saplings and an elderberry bush. Gravel sprayed and pinged the sides of the car. Dust swirled. He braked hard again, but too late to avoid the boulder that appeared in the churned dust.

The right front tire exploded, and the Packard limped to a stop.

Dante jumped from the driver's seat as the dust slowly drifted to the earth again. He twisted around to see the train rolling farther and farther away. *"No!"* His fist found the hood of the car as frustration reverberated through him. He whipped the goggles off his face in passion and fury.

"Think," he commanded himself aloud. Taking a deep breath, he said again, "Come on, think!" Stomping toward the front of the car, he stared at the blown tire and then at the spare fastened to the grill of the car. He reached for it.

The train whistle would have been enough of an announcement, but Oliver Beckett shouted above the noise, "Train from

Forge Rock arriving on time." Not a traveler stood on the platform. "Next stop, Sterling."

Oliver, who was in his early thirties, carried most of his weight in his chest and belly. Short black hair crowned his nearly pretty features. His mother came from Spain, and he had her coloring—but not her grace, for he lumbered along like a boxer ready to punch an opponent.

Being the only employee of the Elder-Locke Railroad posted in Victor City, Oliver took his job seriously. Take the matter of his vest—or vests; he owned two. He wore the black vest while conducting and the maroon vest while selling tickets, and he never performed either task while wearing the wrong-colored vest.

Tense and irritable, that's what Lauralee Murphy thought while observing Beckett from her perch on the courthouse steps. She'd read her uncle's medical digest on behavioral disorders and concluded that Oliver's peculiar management of clothing stemmed from a psychological disturbance.

Either that, or he was a demented lollipop.

"Do you want to distract Oliver while I hide his maroon vest?" Piper asked between licks of her ice cream cone.

"We won't get away with it," Lauralee told her. "He still distrusts me."

"Because you practically killed him with a croquet mallet."

"It was an accident . . . and partially his fault. If he hadn't been breathing down my neck when I took my shot, I wouldn't have hit him."

Piper nodded. "Standing ten feet away is too close."

That was why they were best friends. Piper always saw Lauralee's side of things.

Finished with her cone, Piper smoothed the skirt of her blue dress. "I've had my lunch. What shall we do now?"

"I don't know, but it seems I'm forgetting something." Lauralee brought her knees to her chest and encircled them with her forearms. The late June sun warmed her buckskin riding pants and red-checkered shirt.

"Why are you loitering on the steps of this great legislative building?!"

The deafening query came from behind and above them, and both young women jumped to their feet. With her hand on her heart, Lauralee said, "Hello, Judge Mitchell. I thought I recognized your serene voice."

"Shouldn't you be in school?" He held an ear horn to his head and leaned in from two steps above them.

Piper raised her voice an octave. "We graduated two years ago. You gave the opening remarks."

"But you're only sixteen." The snaps on his vest strained to remain closed, and the white fabric of his shirt poked through the bulging spaces. He looked as if he wobbled there on the steps, and if he fell he'd roll all the way into the street like a big bouncy ball.

"We're twenty, sir."

"Twenty?! By thunder, you should be married with a pack of children around your skirts!"

Lauralee wished he would speak up. *Someone the next town over might not have heard that last bit.* "That's very backward thinking, Judge. Haven't you heard of women's suffrage?"

He descended one step and confided, "Oh, I've suffered all right. I've been married to the same woman for forty years."

"And God bless her," Piper contributed.

"Now, how are your parents?" the judge bellowed at Lauralee. "Are they still on the campaign trail?"

"They'll be home on Sunday. Papa wants to look in on the new colts."

"When he wins the governor's chair, he'll have to put aside such niceties as colts. He'll have to sell the ranch."

His words hit a nerve, and Lauralee glowered at him. "Of course he won't. He'll never sell Long Winter Ranch."

"Of course he will," the old man argued good-naturedly, patting her on the arm and descending the steps. *"Good-bye to you. Go find husbands and get off the street!"* Lauralee's fists landed on her hips. "Of all the . . . If I had a banana peel, I would throw it at his feet."

"I know. All that rubbish about finding husbands . . ."

"I'm talking about the rubbish of my father selling Long Winter Ranch."

Piper leaned on the railing. "Never mind. The judge doesn't know anything about it."

"But what if he does? My father, I mean. What if he does sell the ranch? I don't want to live in Denver. It's dirty and smelly."

Piper crossed her arms. "Has your father said he was going to sell the ranch?"

"No."

"Has he sold any of the stock?"

Lauralee shook her head. "He bought some new horses two months ago."

"Has your mama said anything? Has she started to pack things away?"

"No."

"Well, then," Piper finished, "it is my opinion that your father has no intention of selling the ranch. I think. Maybe you'd better ask him."

Lauralee nodded and turned her face toward the train station. She'd seen movement and focused on the dais.

A woman stepped off the train. Her gray hair hung long

down her back, and she wore a purple skirt and a white billowy blouse. Bangles covered her wrists and forearms. She looked like a gypsy, in her bare feet. Glancing left and right, the woman moved toward the ticket window.

"There you are," a male voice called to Lauralee, interrupting her study. "Did you forget to meet me at Uncle Todd's?" It was her brother, Rick, and he stood at the bottom of the courthouse steps.

Lauralee glanced at Piper. "That's what I forgot."

"How could you possibly forget a thing like that?"

Rick said, "I wanted to give you a list of supplies to buy before I come to get you on Sunday."

"Why can't you buy them?"

"Because I didn't bring the buggy." He placed one booted foot on the first step. "Why are you loafing around out here?" Sunshine brightened his auburn hair. Rick Murphy was two years older than Lauralee, and he looked like their father, with his square jaw. He had their mother's sky-blue eyes though, which caused every ninny in town to fan herself excessively.

"We're not loafing," Piper defended, fanning excessively. "We're watching the train come in."

"No one comes in on the train on Tuesdays."

"Someone did today," Lauralee told him, and took a quick look at the platform again. "A gypsy woman."

"Gypsy," he said with his predictable expression of disapproval. "That's all we need around here, isn't it? You'll go partners with her so she can read your palm and take your money."

Lauralee brightened. "You think she can read palms?"

"No, I do not."

She met him at the bottom of the steps and told him sweetly, "Stop growling. A gypsy can't take my money when I have no money."

It was probably the wrong thing to say.

"What happened to the money I gave you last week?"

"I spent it?"

"On what?"

She shrugged and refolded the list in her hands. "Er . . . ice cream."

"You spent five dollars on a cone?"

"She eats a lot," Piper said, trying to rescue her. She descended the steps and stood next to Lauralee. "Don't you see how much weight she's gained? That's why she had to buy a new dress."

Rick's brows shot skyward. "You bought another dress?"

"I did," Lauralee answered and glared at her treacherous and soon-to-be ex-best friend.

"Pa and I already built another closet for your growing wardrobe."

Thinking fast, she changed the subject. "Has Pa said anything to you about selling the ranch?"

His expression didn't change much except that he appeared slightly confused. "No."

"Judge Mitchell just told me that Pa would sell Long Winter Ranch if he wins the governorship."

His pale eyes held hers. "Simple child, do you believe everything you hear? I worry about you. I really do. You're quite gullible. Do you know that?"

"I am not."

Thunderclouds rolled across his face again. "Yes, you are, and if you think I'm going to give you another penny for these supplies, you're wrong . . . and stop that smirking."

Kissing him on the cheek, she asked, "What do you think we have credit at the store for, anyway?" She spun away from him and walked toward the west road.

Piper caught up to her. "The man is so . . . passionate. Does he ever mention me?"

"Mention you?"

"Does he ever comment that my hair isn't so much red as it is strawberry blond and that my green eyes could be mistaken for jewels?"

Lauralee stopped walking and eyed her friend.

Piper shrugged. "You know, that sort of thing."

"No." They waited for a buggy to roll by before stepping into the wide gravel road. "And why did you tell him I bought a new dress?"

She twisted her lips, trying to delay the answer. "I panicked."

Lauralee rounded on her, and they stood in the middle of the road. "You promised me that you wouldn't utter a word about it."

"I didn't . . . I mean, I won't . . . ever again." Piper followed Lauralee toward the boardwalk. "I don't understand why people can't know you bought a dress for Samantha Brewer. It was a nice thing you did, and maybe Rick wouldn't nag you so much if he knew how charitable you are." They were a quarter of the way to the side of the road.

An automobile squealed around the north bend, rattled over Naberling Bridge, and roared toward the train depot. Out of its grille stuck thick branches with leaves still attached. It looked as though the car had eaten an entire tree and had yet to pick its teeth. The whole of it wobbled and lurched and smoked like a giant metal creature—and it charged Lauralee.

Dante slammed the brakes as fear leaped into his chest. A young woman in a checkered blouse simply stood there in the middle of the road, waiting to get hit by his car.

The engine died as the car skidded to a stop. By the feel of things, he hadn't hit her, but it was hard to see with all the gravel dust stirring in the air. Dante jumped from the car and raced to the front of it. There she still stood, cringing as if waiting for impact. Of all the simpletons in the world!

The train whistle shrieked. Dante's heart pounded. He had to get to the platform . . . Pouncing forward, he hit his knee on the bumper of the car, and he stumbled left. And what, now she comes to life? Dust still lingered, but he saw her wide blue stare. She shied backward at the same time he sprang forward.

What a pretty dance they had, mostly elbows and slapping hands. Then in menacing impatience, Dante grabbed the woman by the shoulders and shouted, *"Out of my way!"* Releasing her, he bolted for the dais.

The air had cleared on the platform, but not a person stood there. He ran toward the ticket window. Did no one work here? The train engine rumbled as someone fed it wood. The passenger cars squeaked as they began to move away. Dante skirted the side of the small office in time to see the caboose budge forward.

He ran after it, gained on it, nearly had a finger on it . . .

A long cross tie sent him flying off to the right of the tracks. Skidding, he grazed the whole side of his suit in the rocks. It seemed he slid forever, and when he lifted his head to see where he'd landed, Dante realized the caboose was pulling farther and farther away.

"Aighhh!" Slamming the earth with his fist, he thrust himself into a sitting position. That's when he noticed several children in the backyard of a house staring at him. The ball they'd tossed now rolled across the ground and bounced off the trunk of a tree.

Jumping to his feet, he brushed gravel dust from his pants. Curse the train. Curse the girl who'd jumped in his way.

He realized he still wore his goggles. Whipping them off in a fit of temper, he ignored the boys who stared at him. He marched toward the station again and tried to gather what little dignity he had left . . . and then tripped on the same blighted cross tie. Tearing off his suit jacket, Dante thrashed it against the rails over and over.

Wretched train.

Hellcat woman.

Tranquil again, he sauntered toward the station with his coat over his arm.

Lamont's Packard sat crooked in the road. A small crowd of townsfolk gathered around it. "Think," he instructed himself aloud as he stood outside the ticket office. The Packard wouldn't make it to the next town—wherever that was. Dante didn't even know where *he* was . . . He gazed at the numerous stone and brick buildings within his sight: saloon, courthouse, train station, and schoolhouse. He'd missed Topeka somehow. Had he crossed into Colorado? He peered through the ticket window. *Next stop: Sterling.* Dante had never heard of it. But this wasn't Sterling; this was Hinterland, or Podunk. Could he hope for a telegraph office?

Stepping off the boardwalk, he avoided the gathered admirers that flocked around the car. Perhaps if he told the telegraph agent that he was a lawyer—and he was, by God—the agent would query Sterling's depot to check if Emelina had arrived there. Maybe the Sterling police would hold on to her until Dante arrived.

Unless Emelina got off the train here . . .

He studied the wide streets and shops on the eastern side of town. Probably he could ask the local police to help him in the same manner. Gypsies were a suspicious lot and as long as the police didn't know that Dante, too, was evading the suspicions of law enforcement in Omaha, they might help him. He looked at the Packard again and the inquisitors there, and then he turned and walked away.

When the dust settled, Lauralee realized that she faced the courthouse. "Who was that?" She twisted around to find Piper.

With an awestruck look of delight, her friend answered, "I don't know, but leave it to you to meet him first."

"Meet him? I never saw him coming . . . What was on his face?"

"Goggles, and even with them on, he's very handsome."

"Is he?" Lauralee glanced at the ticket window, but the man had gone.

"Swarthy, that's what I would call him."

"Well, what does that mean? Is he a pirate?" Lying in the gravel was the slip of paper that Rick had given her, and she bent to pick it up off the ground. Her hands still trembled. An automobile had nearly struck her! Glancing at it now, she saw the limbs sticking out of the grille and noticed the crooked way it leaned in the road. She'd never seen a car up close before today. Somehow she'd expected something more splendid.

Piper had gone so silent that Lauralee glanced at her; she still stared at the dais. "What's the matter?" Lauralee asked her.

"Tell me if I'm seeing things. Is that a monkey?"

"Pardon?"

"There," she said, pointing toward the platform. "Over there."

Lauralee turned. Yep, it was a monkey all right. Not that she'd ever actually seen one, but the animal was fairly unmistakable. It looked like the one illustrated in her third-grade reader. This one wasn't an organ grinder, however, though it did sport a maroon vest.

Piper asked, "What is a monkey doing in Victor City?"

"Obviously it came in with the gypsy."

"I didn't see a gypsy."

Lauralee studied her friend. "The gypsy who got off the train. Honestly, Piper, do you ever notice anything you're supposed to notice?"

"I noticed the monkey," Piper pointed out. "What do you suppose we ought to do?"

That was a tough question, and Lauralee scratched her collarbone in thought. Should they let the monkey mind his own affairs, or should they help him find his owner?

For his part, the monkey didn't look uneasy about being on his own. He did, however, seem slightly confused about where in town to visit first: the church, the courthouse, Marigold's Kitchen . . .

A fairly easy choice: Big Buck's Saloon.

Off the dais, the monkey landed in the pansies, cut across the alley, and climbed onto the boardwalk. He peered beneath the doors of the tavern. When a man stepped out, the monkey scampered inside.

"Buck will have a fit," Piper said, climbing the steps to Buck's place.

Lauralee peeked over the slats and into the semidark room. Laughter drifted on the smoky air. She started to step inside, but Piper touched her arm. "We can't go in there. Someone will see us and Paulette will never invite me to one of her oyster parties."

"You don't like oysters, and you don't like Paulette," Lauralee reminded her, and she stepped into the barroom.

"But I like parties."

Lauralee's eyes slowly adjusted to the new surroundings. Two men played billiards at a table in the middle of the room. Ben Traber thumped on the piano against the far wall. He switched the tune to "The Man on the Flying Trapeze." Four men leaned at the bar, and they appeared dust-covered even in the shadowy light. Several fellows rolled chuck-al-luck dice at one table while others played draw poker at another.

"You girls got exactly five seconds to get out of here!"

The joyous clamber of the tavern died.

Big Buck stood well over six feet and weighed nearly three hundred pounds. The bartender was one of the original settlers in Victor City. The stage depot workers swore the saloon was already open when they built their place. *He came out of the wilderness,* they said. *He's one of the Roma,* others claimed, because Maurice "Big Buck" Lamar had olive coloring and black eyes. What was left of his hair was gray, and it ringed the bald spot atop his head. His nose dominated his face unless he smiled, and then his two front teeth stuck out the most. "I'll skin both of you alive if you stand there one more minute."

"But there's a monk . . ."

"No 'buts.' Vamoose."

Men gawked at them. Billy Yank set down his playing cards and scooted backward to get a better look. "Isn't that one of the Murphy girls?" he asked the fellow next to him.

Axel Garvey spit a wad out the back door. He hollered to Buck, "I didn't know you were adding girls to your payroll, Buck. Are you turning upstairs into a sweet'nin' room?"

"Shut your yap, Garvey," Buck said, setting a crate on the bar. That was when something must have touched his leg, because the old bartender jerked and looked at the floor. His eyes widened, and his jaw dropped.

A screeching noise came from behind the bar.

Buck cleared the counter gracefully but knocked over a table as he shot into the middle of the room. The four men at the bar followed him and formed a line on the opposite side of the room. "What's going on?" Billy Yank demanded, peeking over Buck's shoulder. Axel Garvey stood next to him.

Buck said, "A hairy creature grabbed my leg." With a stout heart, he took a step toward the bar.

The line of men stepped with him.

A tinkering noise sounded, bottles knocked together, and then the monkey hopped onto the bar with a decanter of Scotch in his grip. He thumped it hard on the wood.

Buck and the men took a step backward.

"Man alive," Peter Bennett let out, dropping his cue stick on the floor. "What is that?"

Obviously he'd never read his third-grade literature.

Lauralee clarified. "It's a *monkey.*"

Big Buck eyed her. "You've got something to do with it coming in here, don't you? You know I don't allow beasts of any sort in my establishment."

"Then how come you allowed Chain-Gang Charlie in here the other day?" Axel wanted to know. Most of the men laughed, seeming to forget the monkey squatting on the bar until the animal let out a chattering wail.

Buck roared, *"Lauralee, get him out of here!"*

"Me?"

"Yes, you. That's why you came in here, isn't it? You lost your monkey."

No one had ever accused her of such a thing, and Lauralee thought she might be offended. "It's not *my* monkey."

The animal grew agitated and jumped up and down on the bar. He chattered at the men and waved his fist menacingly. Buck pulled a Colt pistol from his belt, cocked the hammer, and pointed it at the beast. The monkey instantly quieted and lifted his arms in surrender. "Well, stick an apple on my head and let an arrow fly," Buck said in wonderment. "He knows I mean business." His dark eyes found Lauralee's. "Where did you get him?"

"He came in on the train," Piper explained.

Lauralee focused on her. "Actually the gypsy came in on the train. I don't . . ."

"Well, what did Oliver Beckett have to say about that?" Buck wanted to know.

Piper shook her head. "We didn't talk to Oliver, but he must've allowed it because the monkey is wearing his ticket-selling vest."

Lauralee noticed that the monkey did wear a maroon vest, and it was far too large for him. The vest must belong to Oliver.

Axel Garvey said, "Maybe the gypsy woman turned Beckett into a monkey."

Now, by most people's standards, the idea was ludicrous.

"The gypsy woman . . . ," the men murmured in awe. "Poor Oliver . . ."

"Oh, come on," Lauralee said sternly. "Be reasonable."

"I say we go over to the train depot and find Oliver," Peter Bennett suggested. "Then we'll know for sure whether this hairy beast is Beckett or not."

"Now that's being reasonable," Buck insisted. He waved the pistol at the monkey and pointed toward the exit. To everyone's surprise, the animal jumped from the bar and headed for the door.

As everyone filed out of Buck's, Lauralee paused to wonder how things had so quickly got off beam and awry. All she'd meant to do was warn Buck that he had a monkey in his saloon, and now she was swept along in a Beckett-hunting posse.

Maybe if she stayed in the middle of the crowd no one, and by no one she meant her brother, Rick, would see her. Stepping off the boardwalk, she rushed to keep stride with Axel and Billy.

This was not her being gullible! She didn't believe the gypsy had cursed Oliver, but Lauralee did, however, have three questions in her mind: One, did the monkey belong to the gypsy, and if so, two, where was the gypsy, and three . . . exactly how much did a palm reading cost, anyway?

On the station platform, the men scattered in search of Oliver. Big Buck and Peter Bennett tapped on the ticket window. Lauralee and Piper leaned against the Packard still sitting crooked in the road. No one else was about. Those who'd gathered around the car had gone back to work. "This is ridiculous, you know."

"I know," Piper answered, nodding her red head. "Having a train station open all hours when the trains come only once a day is absurd."

"I meant looking for Oliver. That is what's ridiculous."

Piper raised a brow and answered softly, "Oh."

The sun cleared the morning clouds, and the courthouse flag waved limply in the soft breeze. Marigold's Kitchen served lunch, and Lauralee could smell roasted beef. Across the road, she saw Judge Mitchell again. He helped his wife out of a day carriage as another woman sat inside the buggy waiting for a hand. Farther along were the mill and the smithy buildings. Every corner of town stirred with activity.

But no one manned the train depot.

Buck stood in the middle of the dais, still holding the monkey at gunpoint. "I say we split into twos and search the town."

Lauralee and Piper shrugged at each other and began on the east side of town. Victor City had originally been built on a single graveled road that ran north and south out of the Col-

orado foothills. Now the road curved eastward over the Naberling Creek Bridge and cut southward again. New businesses
lined both sides of the extension. Piper searched for Oliver in
the pharmaceutical while Lauralee checked inside Celia's Department Store, where she immediately was distracted by a
display of bonnets and sun hats. Afterward, they searched the
library together and then stepped inside the Victor City Church.

Reverend Carmichael closed a door and then turned in surprise to see Lauralee and Piper. "And what are you fine ladies
doing today? Are you glorifying God in your adventures, or are
you, like so many people in this town, running amok like chim-
panzees?"

It was his little joke for the day.

"It's funny you should mention a monkey," Lauralee told
him with her hand on the back of a wooden pew; two rows of
six faced a beautifully carved pulpit. Behind the pulpit was a
choir loft with forty chairs. Forty had always seemed ambitious
to Lauralee for a town of one hundred and thirty-three, especially since the Presbyterian church also met weekly, in what
used to be the sheriff's office.

Carmichael stepped into the aisle. Thick gray hair sat curled
on top of his head. "I mentioned a monkey?"

"You said 'chimpanzee.' "

"I merely used a euphemism to describe the condition of
fallen man. Why did you mention a monkey?"

"One came in on the train today," Piper told him.

Lauralee shook her head. "A gypsy came in on the train. We
saw the monkey at the depot."

"After the train came and went," Piper concluded and gazed
at the reverend. "So, do you see my logic?"

He nodded. "Did you invite the monkey to the Presbyterian
church for Sunday service?"

"We should have," Lauralee said with a grin. "Its first inclination was to visit the saloon." She leaned on the pew. "Have you seen Oliver Beckett? We're looking for him."

"So is God, my dear. So is God."

Outside again, Lauralee told Piper, "I'll bet Oliver is back to work. Someone probably found him in Marigold's. It's lunchtime."

Piper walked on Lauralee's left side and she paused when they were even with the police station. "Oh, my goodness," she said, staring in the window. "There he is." Wrapping her arm into Lauralee's, Piper pulled her inside.

Chapter Three

Five deputies maintained law in Victor City and kept the town free of juvenile delinquents, pickpockets, violators of the Sunday laws, and those who kept a disorderly house. Reuben Shank had been elected chief of police. He was the man to reckon with if a body stole or rabble-roused. He stood six foot six, outweighed Big Buck by fifty pounds, and had a fleshy ruddy face and small blue eyes.

Though Shank's appearance demanded attention, he wasn't the first person Lauralee noticed when she stepped into the building. Just beyond the pine counter was *not* Oliver Beckett, as Lauralee imagined Piper meant when she pulled her into the station, but the man who'd nearly driven over her at the train depot. It wasn't as though she recognized him instantly but he was swarthy, just as Piper described. Black hair, olive complexion, and square jaw made him appear daredevilish indeed.

Suddenly, his bold and flashing eyes fastened on her. He puckered his brow, as if trying to place her, and then said, "There's the girl who fouled my search."

Lauralee glanced over her shoulder. Since no one stood

there, she had to presume the man spoke of her. She faced him again, delighted, and ready to enter the spirit of the argument—if someone would just give her an idea of what was going on. "What did I do?"

"What you *ought* to do is get thrown in jail for obstructing justice."

Oh, she liked him. There he stood so virtuously, defending himself so arduously against the wrongs in the world that a woman just *had* to fall in love with him.

Reuben Shank's large profile blocked her view suddenly as he moved around the counter, took Lauralee's arm, and dragged her forward to face her accuser. "This fellow is attorney Dante Quinn from San Francisco. He has issue with you, Lauralee. Did you or did you not purposely step in his way when he tried to reach the train?"

"Didn't you run into me?" she asked the glorious Quinn. He smelled of wind and rubber and mud . . .

"You were in the middle of the road."

She enjoyed his voice. It was baritone, and rich, and wholly in keeping with his appearance. "I was on the *side* of the road."

"You came to life just when I ran for the platform."

Lauralee didn't care for the way he'd said *came to life,* as though she were a storefront dummy. She retorted, "Small wonder, since you charged me with those bug-eyed goggles. I thought you were a giant bug." She smiled pleasantly after saying it. There was nothing like a little bantering to freshen up a girl.

Rueben Shank pulled her aside. "All right, there's no reason to squabble. Mr. Quinn, we'll let you know what we hear from Sterling. Where are you staying?"

Still eyeing Lauralee, Quinn asked Shank, "Will you direct

me to your local boardinghouse?" His gaze shifted to the chief.

"Blue Bells is on the west street. Cross the bridge, and you'll see it."

Without further argument, Mr. Quinn nodded and walked out the office door. Lauralee twisted back around to stare at Chief Shank. "He said I fouled his search. What is he searching for?"

"It's not your business."

"Is it a monkey?"

The chief wrinkled his features in wonderment. "He didn't mention a monkey."

"I only ask because Buck is holding one captive at gunpoint."

Shank nodded. "That's fine. As long as everything is under control." It was his way of staying out of trivial matters. A man like Reuben Shank concerned himself with hard crime. "Now stop asking a lot of questions," he told her. "And stay away from Dante Quinn."

Stay away from Dante Quinn indeed, Lauralee thought as she shut the front door of her uncle's house. Why should she have to stay away from him?

Because not doing so could result in a short jail term.

So, if she were going to figure out what Quinn was up to, she would need to act sneaky about it. This did not necessarily bother her; it just meant that she would have to take a job at Blue Bells and clean rooms until she found clues that would lead her to whomever or whatever it was that Dante Quinn searched for—obviously it was the gypsy woman. She got off the train, Dante Quinn raced for the train, the gypsy disappeared, and Mr. Quinn requested police assistance to locate her.

There, Lauralee had read the tea leaves, and she hadn't mopped a floor or fluffed one pillow to figure it out.

Except, why would a lawyer chase a gypsy to a train depot? Perhaps the woman had witnessed a crime and Quinn needed her testimony. Or maybe the woman was the suspect herself. She ran for a train when Mr. Quinn questioned her regarding the murder . . . Lauralee was in the middle of that theory when the doorbell chimed.

Now, Dante Quinn had no way of knowing that her uncle was the town's physician or he might've tolerated whatever ailed him—or so it seemed by the expression he offered when Lauralee opened the front door. "You're the doctor?"

He said it with such doubt that Lauralee thought to claim that, yes, she was, and how did he suffer knowing he'd called a surgeon a storefront dummy? She didn't voice this; instead, she asked, "May I help you?" without answering his question of whether she was the doctor.

"I'd like to see the physician."

"Then you've come to the right place," she said, enjoying this very much and valuing the enormous potential of the moment. She took a step backward to allow him entry and then shut the door behind him. He'd changed his clothing before coming and stood there wearing a white shirt and brown trousers. His nearly black hair was more wavy than curly, except at the back where it hit his collar. Thankfully, he no longer smelled of rubber and mud, but of fresh greens and woods. "Follow me," Lauralee told him, and she led him beyond the stairway and through the first door on the right. She asked, "Do you have an injury?"

"Surprisingly, no," he answered, suggesting their collision had harmed him in some way.

"Are you ill? Feeling puny, are you?"

"Not at all." It was the smallest movement his eyebrow made, as if he acknowledged her teasing, but the man was terribly straight-faced.

Intriguing.

"Then how may I assist you?"

"Well, *Doctor,*" he said, leaning casually against the examination table and keeping eye contact, "I'd like to ask you a scientific question."

"Shouldn't you ask a scientist a scientific question?"

"Surely you've studied science."

Lauralee couldn't remember ever meeting someone so reserved before, someone who restrained his demeanor as Quinn did. If she hadn't witnessed him rushing for the train depot she would've believed him to be most phlegmatic. But the way he'd grabbed her by the shoulders and shouted "out of my way" had been ardent and quick-tempered.

So, what was Quinn hiding? And what were they talking about again? Oh, yes, science. She said, "Of course a doctor studies science. What is your question?"

"It concerns the laws of heredity."

"Well, you're the lawyer. Shouldn't you know enough about the laws of—whatever?"

He leaned toward her and said, "Heredity . . . characteristics . . . traits . . . does that sound vaguely familiar to you, Doctor?" Though his voice sounded just a hint strained, his features remained completely detached, unaffected.

"Do keep yourself calm, Mr. Quinn. I don't appreciate your emotional outbursts. They are most unseemly."

An amazing thing happened then: Dante Quinn laughed. And the transformation in him was astounding. His dark eyes danced and he had dimples on his cheeks. Teeth. He had teeth, shiny white ones, almost perfectly straight except that the bottom front two overlapped a bit. Lauralee found herself completely smitten with him. "Just for the record," she admitted, "I'm not the doctor."

His grin turned into a smirk and he tilted his head to the side. "Ah, yes, let the record show that you're being truthful at last."

"My uncle is the doctor."

"Todd Thomas, right?" He pointed to a framed certificate above the supply cabinet, to the left of the books. "His physician's license is there."

She glanced to where he pointed. "So you knew it all along? You were playing with me?"

"I knew it all along without seeing the certificate."

"What gave it away?" she asked. "The fact that I didn't know the laws of heredity?"

He shook his head. "Chief Shank. He would've introduced you as 'Doctor So-and-So' instead of 'Laura.' "

"Lauralee," she corrected. "Lauralee Murphy."

"That's very pretty . . . as you are."

He didn't say it in a flirtatious tone. It was as though he simply stated his judgment to the court. Hmm. Movement in the hallway caught her eye. "Uncle Todd," she called. "You have a patient."

Todd Thomas stepped into the room and shook Dante Quinn's hand. "Ill are you?" He lifted his chin and peered through his spectacles. His blond hair fell straight over his brow. "What ails you, young man?"

"Yes, what ails you?" asked Lauralee.

Seeming to recognize Quinn's restraint, Todd turned to Lauralee. "Barney Crowe needs a three-quarter bandage. Will you see to it?"

She moved toward the door just as Dante said, "I merely have a question regarding the laws of heredity."

"Mendel's or Erich Von Tschermak's?" Todd asked. "Well, it doesn't matter. They both said the same thing, but Mendel clearly demonstrated the independence of selected characters and their free combining of offspring in accordance with probabilistic laws . . ." He turned to pull a book from the shelf.

From the doorway, Lauralee smiled at Quinn. She said, "And here I thought you came to find out about the gypsy."

Dante's dark eyebrows shot upward in surprise. He took a step toward her, but she shut the door quickly, leaving him to his fate with Todd Thomas lecturing about probabilistic laws. And *that* was his due punishment for calling Lauralee an obstructer of justice.

Chapter Four

After shaking Dr. Thomas' hand, Dante stepped out of the room and paused by the staircase. He could see Lauralee Murphy through the sheer curtains over the front window. She rocked on the porch swing.

He'd had a curious reaction to her in the doctor's office. She was pretty, but that wasn't what struck him, not entirely, anyway. He'd seen many beautiful women in his lifetime. He supposed it was her good nature that appealed to him. Cheerful people were always his favorite sort—most probably because he didn't have that specific trait himself. Dante wished he could be more cheerful. He longed to strike up a conversation with someone without his suspicious nature coming into play. His skeptical disposition was what made him a good law student, yet there were times he wished he wasn't as good at edicts and rules and was better at interacting with people.

It reassured him to know Lauralee had seen Emelina; it meant Emelina got off the train here in Victor City. How Lauralee knew he was looking for the woman, Dante didn't know. It didn't matter. What mattered was that Lauralee knew in which direction Emelina had headed.

He meant to question Lauralee. She obviously waited for him there on the swing. She'd baited him in hopes that he would find her. What was in her mind? he wondered. Perhaps she was eager for an adventure. She certainly seemed the type of person who liked to figure it all out and solve the riddle of the day. Dante was a lot like that himself. His advantage over her was that he'd studied law for five years and had become expert at questioning the witness. With that assurance, he moved toward the door, turned the knob, and stepped out onto the porch.

He approached the swing.

In an attempt at brilliance, and with the effort to put the witness at ease, Dante stated, "I now know more about pea plants and chromosomes than any man has a right to know."

"That makes you the luckiest person ever," Lauralee said, rocking on the swing with one foot on the floor. She'd tucked her other foot beneath her leg. Dante appreciated the fall of her hair that turned different shades of blond in the sunlight behind her. She asked him, "Why do you want to know about heredity?"

"Heredity was only part of my question for Dr. Thomas."

A buggy rolled by the front of the house. Its turning wheels whirled the hot dust in the street, and the noise of the axle squeaking caused Dante to move closer to the swing. He prompted, "Now, if I may, I'd like to ask you a question."

"As you've previously discovered, I know nothing about science . . . Would you care to sit?" She moved to the left of the seat to make room for him.

Dante remained where he stood. An attorney always stood

when questioning a testifier. "It's not a scientific question. Will you tell me about the gypsy?"

"I don't know anything about her."

"Didn't you say in the doctor's room that you'd seen the gypsy, Miss Murphy?" If she meant to toy with him, Dante would object firmly.

"Please call me Lauralee."

He had learned to refer to the deponent in the proper manner and said, "I prefer Miss Murphy." Dante saw the way Lauralee drew her eyebrows together as though he'd offended her in some fashion. He couldn't imagine how; he'd kept his voice amiable. "Didn't you say you saw a gypsy?"

"Goodness," she said with a breathy laugh. "Have we been transported to a courtroom?" Her eyes lit with amusement. It was then that Dante knew they were gray, rather than blue. They reminded him of the San Francisco Bay.

It didn't matter that she was attractive. *Think,* Dante instructed himself. To Lauralee, he asked, "You're teasing me, is that it? I must say that I don't appreciate your coyness, Miss Murphy. You have no idea how important it is that I find this woman."

She still appeared delighted, as though she found something amusing about his behavior. "I'm sorry," she offered politely. "I wasn't trying to sound coy."

"Then answer my question."

There it was again, the pulling of the brows, as if she were nettled at his tone. "I don't know anything about her. I saw a woman who resembled a gypsy. She got off the train."

"Did she return to the train?"

"I don't know. My brother took that moment to shout at me."

"I can well imagine," Dante said, not bothering to keep the note of irritation out of his voice. He twisted around to see the train station. All looked quiet. Didn't anyone work there? "Did you see which way she headed?"

"Toward the ticket window."

He turned to peer at Lauralee again. She stood now and the porch swing rocked gently behind her. He asked, "Did anyone else see her?"

"Since I am not the only one with eyesight in this town, I imagine someone else saw her. Although I wouldn't ask my brother, nor my friend Piper, for they both are quite blind today."

Dante had no idea what she meant. Frustrated, he walked toward the steps. "Very well, Miss Murphy. If you see her, will you tell me?" When she didn't answer quickly, he glanced at her over his shoulder.

She smiled courteously. "Of course, Mr. Quinn."

What to make of the man, Lauralee didn't know. In Uncle Todd's office, he'd acted amiable and almost charming, but when he stepped outside, he'd switched to bullying in his legal questioning. Dante Quinn certainly had a lot to learn about the art of cajolement.

She leaned on the porch rail and watched the road. A soft breeze stirred sunflower vine leaves on the arbor. Inside Victor City Bank, Winston Reed stuck his long face near the window, turned over the sign in the glass to read CLOSED, and flipped the blinds shut. Lauralee gazed northward toward the large clock in front of the depot. *Five minutes after four.* Shoot, Lauralee didn't need a clock to tell her what the time was; Winston closed the bank at the same moment every day when the grumbling started in his stomach. Movement caught her attention. The monkey, still wearing the maroon vest, shambled out of the saloon and filled a pail of water at the pump next to the building. Had Buck taught it to do that?

CJ Love

Her eyes wandered to the spaces between the buildings. Where was the Roma woman? Maybe she had returned to the train and left town. But why would she disembark if she were only going to get on the train again?

Dante Quinn had proved one thing to her, Lauralee thought as her mind went full circle from the monkey to the gypsy and back to Quinn, and that was that beneath his courtly exterior he was an intensely frustrated man. This whole issue was more than a legal matter to him.

She moved toward the door and stepped inside the house, meaning to start dinner for her uncle and cousin. What had Quinn said? *Heredity was only part of my question for Dr. Thomas.*

Well, what was the other part?

In the kitchen, Lauralee pulled a pot off the rack. She would ask her uncle the question conversationally. If she inquired in a roundabout way, Uncle Todd might share Mr. Quinn's questions with her. And if he didn't, then it was off to Blue Bells for a scullery job.

They ate dinner in the kitchen, since it was only the three of them. Lauralee served Boston baked beans and corn bread. Todd sat near the window, with Lauralee across the small table, and Daniel, Todd's eleven-year-old son, sat between them. Lauralee considered how she might broach the subject of Dante Quinn when Daniel said, "Don't you think Caroline is the prettiest name you've ever heard?" He spoke to Lauralee and put a large spoonful of beans into his mouth.

"Caro*line* or Caro*lynn?*"

"Caro*line.*"

"Who is Caroline?" Todd wanted to know, studying the boy

over the rim of his glasses. He still wore his black medical coat with a dark shirt beneath it.

"Caroline Petrova. Her family moved from Massachusetts, and today they came into town."

Lauralee nodded. "And we're eating *Boston* baked beans in her honor."

Todd asked, "You know the Petrovas?"

"No, I'm pointing out the coincidence that they're from Massachusetts and we're eating Boston . . . never mind." She took a bite of corn bread.

Todd glanced at his son. "Petrova. That sounds like a Russian name."

"Caroline's brother told me that their grandfather moved here from Russia. Their father is a jeweler."

Lauralee perked up. "A jeweler . . . how fascinating."

Todd and Daniel stared at her. Todd asked, "What's so fascinating about that?"

"Maybe he'll open a shop."

"Their mama is sick," Daniel told Lauralee as if it had some bearing on Mr. Petrova opening a jewelry store. The male mind was an unpredictable thing, Lauralee believed, and she tried to stay with the boy's flow of thought. "They were on their way to Alaska when it happened and they bought the Thompsons' old house near the Becketts." He dug into his food again. Daniel didn't look like his father, except for the spectacles perched atop his nose. He looked like his mom, Mary, who had died four years previously. Daniel had her wiry hair and round face.

His father asked, "Do you know what ails Mrs. Petrova?"

"Caroline didn't say."

Lauralee thought if Daniel said *Caroline* once more she

would bonk him on the head with her spoon. She changed the subject. "Does Dante Quinn have some fatal disease?"

Todd frowned. "No, of course not." He set his spoon aside and wiped his mouth with his napkin. "He asked about the laws of heredity."

"So he fears catching some fatal disease from his relatives?"

"I'm not at liberty to say, but he mentioned an interesting idea. The idea that crime might be linked in families."

"Can it?" both Lauralee and Daniel asked together.

"There's no *crime* gene, no. Now, if a man or a woman were raised in a family of thieves, he or she would be likely to re-peat the behavior, but a bent toward crime is not inherited. Mental illness can be inherited . . ."

"He's mentally ill," Lauralee stated, as if she'd solved a puzzle.

Todd's brow wrinkled further, and he pushed at his glasses. "Who?"

"Dante Quinn."

"Of course he's not. What a thing to suggest."

"You brought it up," she defended.

"No, he didn't. You did," Daniel reminded her. "You asked him if Dante Quinn had a fatal illness, and Papa won't tell you why he visited."

Many curses on the boy's hairsplitting memory! She changed the subject again. "So the Petrovas bought the old Thompson place near the Becketts? Has either of you seen Oliver today?"

"I saw him on my way to the Wheelers' house."

"But not on your way home?"

Daniel turned excitedly toward his father. "Did you know Buck has a monkey?"

"I think it came to town with the gypsy," Lauralee chimed in.

"Gypsy," Todd snapped, lifting his spoon again. "That's all

we need around here." He pointed the utensil at Lauralee. "You're not allowed to partner with a gypsy. She'll take all your money."

Apparently there really was something to the laws of heredity, she thought, spooning beans into her mouth. Uncle Todd and her brother Rick had the same *nagging* gene.

The evening had turned sticky as well as warm. To the southwest, towering clouds rose above the mountain ranges. Anyone who lived north of the Rockies recognized the foul weather. The storm looked a day away and depending on how wide it spread, Victor City would see rain.

Lauralee loved to take in the sky. She supposed she'd caught her father's fondness for it. When Wade Murphy was home, he would sit on White Basker Knoll and watch the stars come out. Ever since Lauralee could remember, she sat with him. At a young age, she'd learned to recite *clear moon, frost soon; a wind in the south has rain in her mouth;* and *when the swallows fly low a storm is gonna blow.*

The street lamp at the corner of the road flickered just as Lauralee pushed on the gate. She thought to visit Piper and her mother, Rosemarie McKinney, who lived northeast of Naberling Creek Bridge and right next to the schoolhouse where Mrs. McKinney taught first through twelfth grade. It was seven o'clock by railroad time when Lauralee stepped onto the road.

Dante stood on the porch of Blue Bell's Tenement, watching not the sky but the town. The lights from the barroom spilled out onto the street and brightened the north road, but the south end of town remained in shadows. Lamont's car no longer sat in front of the train depot. Dante had paid three teenaged boys to help him push the Packard behind the tenement house. He intended to ask a tradesman to look at the engine and tire. Meanwhile, he would keep constant watch for Emelina.

Why had she come to this town? Did she know someone here, someone who would hide her away for a time? It seemed unlikely. Gypsies traveled together. Whole families lived in wagons, not in well-manicured communities like Victor City. Dante had never seen a town quite as clean and flowery as this one. A weed wouldn't live daylight to dark.

The light in front of the train station flickered to life at the same time he heard a gate hinge squeak. Dante gazed toward the south. For a moment, he saw no one, but then he recognized the figure of Lauralee Murphy. She stopped and spoke to an older couple in the middle of the road. Obviously, people liked her, and she must have grown up in this town. She would be able to tell him if any Roma lived nearby.

Questioning her earlier had not turned out the way he'd hoped. She considered him more entertaining than stern. Maybe if he chose a different approach with her, Lauralee would take him seriously. But Dante didn't necessarily want to confide in her.

He didn't trust her not to tell the entire town that Dante Quinn was a cursed man who stole jewels in his sleep . . . He placed a hand on his stomach, which suddenly burned when he thought of his plight. It took all of his self-control not to run into the woods, screaming and jumping around like a wild man.

Laughter caused him to look again at the threesome in the street. Lauralee laughed too, and the old man raised his hand in farewell to her. How delightful for them all, Dante thought. Their lives were free and unadorned by gypsies and hexes. He used to live like that as well. And if he could find Emelina and talk reasonably to her—less any scarves she might float at him—he could go back to his quiet, well-ordered life. Then he too would imagine striking up conversations with oldsters on the street and talking about the weather and whatnot.

Then again, he'd never had the temperament for such niceties. Dante had always been somewhat envious of people who were free-spirited enough to talk to anyone about anything. Lauralee seemed to be in midconversation with whomever she met. In all probability she never stopped to think about what she said or what others thought of her. Conceivably, he could try an amiable approach with her and find out if any Roma people lived nearby.

Now, if he only knew how to act amiably . . .

With nothing to do but make the effort, Dante pushed off the railing and walked into the road.

"Lauralee Murphy," someone called out behind her. When she turned she saw Dante Quinn. A small thrill joggled her heart; the man was so very handsome. Lamplight from Marigold's Kitchen spread out onto the road, and Lauralee could see his face in the golden shadows. His thick brows slanted over his black, black eyes. He didn't say anything, simply stood before her looking like a superb statue . . . David or Apollo Belvedere, perhaps.

"Hello, Mr. Quinn," she said courteously. "Do you feel the storm building?"

He gazed skyward and into the now darkened heavens. "There's a storm?"

"It will rain tomorrow. Wait and see." A fresh breeze caught her hair, and she brushed it from her cheek.

He nodded, with his dark eyes watching her every move-ment. He remained silent, but it seemed he tried hard to think of what to say next. Lauralee could nearly see the wheels of his mind turning. Finally, he blurted out, "May I buy your supper?"

"I've already eaten my supper, thank you." She couldn't help but smile at him. Lauralee would've never believed Dante Quinn would behave so bashfully. She found it endearing.

He smiled in return and it seemed he relaxed a bit. "Will you sit with me while I eat mine?"

"I've already told you all I know about your gypsy—"

"First," he interrupted, "I don't have a gypsy. Second, my only desire is to have your company for a time."

Beholding his warm eyes, his sculpted features, and his full mouth, Lauralee supposed she could endure his presence for a time. "Very well, Mr. Quinn. I will sit with you."

A mended fire burned low inside the restaurant. Marigold and two other ladies bustled in and out of the swinging doors to the kitchen. At banner speed, food and dishes and lights had been set in order on the table near the window where Dante Quinn and Lauralee sat. The boards gleamed with candles white and golden.

Marigold placed a glass of lemonade in front of Lauralee. "You're sitting in the same spot your mama did the first time I saw her." This was at least the ninety-ninth time Lauralee had heard the story. Marigold continued: "She was the prettiest woman this town had ever seen."

"You look like your mother?" Dante asked as Marigold moved away from the table.

She shook her head. "I look like my father, except for the blond hair."

"Then he's beautiful as well?"

Lauralee laughed at him. "I'm sure he would appreciate your saying so."

Dante tucked into his food and, after a short time, he asked, "Why do you live with your uncle?"

"I don't live with him. My parents are traveling. My brother, Rick, runs the ranch, and I help Uncle Todd while they're gone."

He glanced up from his plate. "Help him?"

"My mother worries over him, since his wife died. I stay to keep him company and to cook for him."

"A faithful sister and niece—how rare."

He said this in a low tone, almost a whisper. At first she thought he meant to compliment her, but then again, Lauralee wasn't sure what he meant. He didn't offer to explain, so she asked, "You were born in San Francisco?"

"Yes, that's right."

"Is that where your family lives?" She lifted her glass of lemonade and took a sip.

"No, but I was born there, in an important house on Nob Hill." He smiled at her.

"Oh, important, was it?"

"My father was a well-known lawyer."

She set the glass on the table. "So you're following in his footsteps?"

"Good God, no," he said and dropped his napkin into his lap again before tearing off a piece of bread from the loaf in the center of the table.

"Is he still alive?"

"No," he told her, swallowing his food. "He went to bed with a bottle of whiskey every night, and one morning he didn't wake up."

"I'm sorry."

"Stop looking at me with those sympathetic blue eyes of yours." He chewed for a long moment. "I'm alone and I like it that way."

"No one likes to be alone."

He narrowed his dark eyes and watched her a moment.

"Don't you believe that, Lauralee. Not everyone has a happy little family like you do."

"Then why did you ask me to sit with you, Mr. Quinn, if you prefer to be alone?"

"I mean to confide in you."

That perked her ears. "Really?"

"The woman I'm searching for caused someone's death. It was unpremeditated, I assume, a selfish act without malice. But I must ask her a series of questions."

"Who is she?"

"Her name is Emelina Istok, and, as you've realized, she is Roma, a gypsy. I followed her here from Omaha."

"I thought you came from San Francisco?"

"Yes," he said with a nod. "But I attended school in Nebraska. Do you know if any Roma people live in the area?"

"Besides Big Buck, you mean?"

"Who is Big Buck?"

"The bartender." She leaned in. "People have always said he was gypsy, but I don't believe it. He's lived above the saloon most of his life. I have seen caravans near Wolf Whistle Creek at harvest time. He has never joined their parties."

"Harvest time. That's still two months away." He gazed across the room, to think a moment, and then his eyes found hers again. "Where is this Wolf Creek? Is it in walking distance?"

"Anywhere is walking distance if you've got a lot of time."

He raised his brow at her answer, and then said, "Do any gypsies live there?"

"No," she told him, wondering at his crestfallen look. "You think she's staying with someone locally?"

He shrugged and placed his napkin on the plate.

She thought for a moment, trying to help him if she could.

"When I was a little girl, there was a caravan of gypsies near Fool's Peak. That was back when people actually traveled that route."

"Where is Fool's Peak?"

"In the mountains southeast of here. It was a mining town, but there was a cave-in years ago, and the place is deserted."

He nodded. "Another long walk?"

"Yes, and I don't think she'd go there alone. No one goes out there . . ."

The bell over the door jingled, and both Lauralee and Dante glanced that direction. Chief Reuben Shank had to turn sideways to get his shoulders through the narrow doorway. When he noticed Dante, he nodded and moved toward the table. "I have news for you, young fella. No one got off the train in Sterling."

Dante pushed out of his chair and stood next to the chief. "Thank you. That means I'll stay in Victor City a little longer than I first thought. I assume your men are keeping their eyes open?"

"You assume correctly," Shank said. He turned toward Lauralee. "I thought I told you to stay away from Mr. Quinn."

She grinned at the police chief. "He practically begged me to have dinner with him."

"Thank you for sitting with me, Lauralee," Dante said, pushing his chair beneath the table. "I don't need you to answer any more questions."

And that was how it felt to be dismissed from the witness stand.

She followed the men out of the restaurant after Dante laid bills on the table to cover the tab. Lauralee pitied the woman who fell in love with Mr. Quinn; the poor wretch would get nothing but a heart full of stipulations and restraining orders. She vowed right then not to be the one who fell for him. Quinn was as chilly hearted as a well digger's ears.

The men moved northward toward the courthouse, and Lauralee watched them for a moment before she crossed the road and walked toward Todd's house. Dante Quinn had said he meant to confide in her, but he hadn't. He was much too reticent to confide in anyone. The clues he'd let slip about his family helped her understand him a little. He'd had an unhappy childhood and now, in response, he behaved distrustfully. Lauralee supposed that made sense. She would look up a passage in Todd's medical tomes when she went inside. For the moment, she sat on the porch swing and rocked back and forth.

Emelina Istok had killed someone, but Dante hadn't said whom she had killed. Maybe she killed his father by encouraging the man to drink . . . That would make this more than a legal case for Mr. Quinn, wouldn't it? Lauralee hadn't gotten the chance to ask Dante about his mother. Maybe the gypsy woman had somehow caused his mother's death. What had he said? *It was unpremeditated, I assume, a selfish act without malice* . . . But how had it come to be that a famous lawyer had been caught up with a Roma woman—or better yet, how had an old Roma woman killed the wife of a San Francisco lawyer?

There were endless possibilities to that scenario, and Lauralee stood and walked toward the front door. She'd have to think on this a bit more before she could even make a good guess at what Dante Quinn was up to in his mad chase of a gypsy.

She woke early to get out of the house on time. The weekly newspaper, *The Victor Gazette,* published overnight on Wednesdays and Lauralee wanted to be the first in line to buy one. There wasn't much of a fashion page, but she loved to read the theater reviews from Denver, and others sometimes from as far away as Chicago or New York. Dressed in a white pouter pigeon blouse and gray trumpet skirt, she departed Uncle Todd's house just as the sun took a first glance across the west road. Shredded clouds painted the sky pink and red.

As it turned out, she wasn't the only one awake. Deputy Efren Vaughn stood near the courthouse steps with his back against the lamppost as he waited for the newspaper cart to arrive. He wore a black shirt and trousers, and his shiny badge glinted in the dawn break. There was a small light on in the train station's office, and Lauralee slowed her pace to peer in that direction. When she stood next to Vaughn, she asked, "Have you seen Oliver Beckett this morning?"

"I wasn't looking for him," he said without turning toward her. His black hair curled around his ears, and he had heavy brows that gave a woman the impression that he was thoughtful, poetic maybe, or romantic.

Lauralee knew better.

"You don't have to look for him to see him," she retorted. They'd never really hit it off, she and Vaughn; it dated back to a spelling bee when Efren forgot to say "capital T" when he spelled "Thanksgiving," and Lauralee had giggled about it.

She had been six! And she couldn't spell Thanksgiving with or without a capital T.

Lauralee might've also made fun of his name, but *Efren?* Who was named Efren, anyhow? But they were grownups now, right? They should be able to put the past behind them.

Efren, however, looked no longer at Lauralee but at the bridge on which Piper half walked, half ran to meet them. He straightened off the post.

Lauralee gazed from Efren to her friend, who wore a pretty

floral bonnet and a long-sleeved white blouse with a wide black velvet belt that showed off her small figure. Vaughn squared his shoulders and cleared his throat.

What was this?

Efren Vaughn smiled and his eyes sparkled as he watched Piper move closer. Evidently the angels sang. Lauralee told him, "You look beautiful, Efren."

He gritted his teeth behind his smile. "Shut up."

A shaft of sunlight perforated the curtains and hit the edge of the bed where Dante lay. Bits of lint spiraled inside the beam, and he watched it a moment while he remembered where he was . . . Bluebells . . . Victor City. Swinging his feet to the floor, he grabbed his pants from near the foot of the bed.

An early start, that's what he needed. Emelina might return to the depot and leave town. If he didn't catch up to her there, he'd search every store, every building, and every alleyway for her.

Voices outside his window caused Dante to pull the curtain aside. He buttoned his shirt while he peered into the road from the top floor. There was Lauralee. She stood out to him always. If a crowd of women stood in the street, he would see her first—because she'd be the one smiling. There didn't seem to be a force on earth that could stop Lauralee from being cheerful. He could see only the side of her face, for she spoke to the man who stood beside her.

It didn't surprise Dante that she was an early riser. His mother had been the first out of bed in the mornings too. She would cook him breakfast before he'd run off to school . . .

What a pleasant memory, Dante realized. His mother had been happy then, or so he'd thought. The house seemed warm when she was there. Lauralee was like that. She would make a house warm with her soft laughter and twinkling gray-blue eyes.

Dante leaned away from the window and hardened his heart. Miss Murphy was just like every other woman he'd ever known: not worth trusting. Turning away, he rubbed his jaw. He hadn't brought his shaving kit with him. He'd left it in the trunk of Lamont's car. He found the key on the dressing table, right next to a pair of diamond earrings.

Someone whispered, "The monkey's gone," behind her. Lauralee turned to find Big Buck standing there. He repeated, "The monkey is gone and Oliver Beckett is back managing the depot."

Gray stubble covered his double chin. Lauralee wondered if Buck had just climbed out of bed, because he wore only a pair of dark trousers over his long johns. "Well, if Oliver is back, then everything's fine," she told him. "And the monkey probably ran off in search of its owner."

"What about the monkey?" Piper asked, finally arriving and standing next in line. Hester Green stood behind Piper, and then Shirley Tate. After her was Tanner Wolfe, who worked at the bank and always bought more papers than necessary just so he could line his trash basket. He was a menace to all who loved the theater.

Buck kept his voice low. "It turned into Oliver again."

"Is he all right?" Piper wanted to know. "Did you ask him how he feels?"

"He's not the monkey," Lauralee told the wind—or she might as well have, for all the attention they paid to her.

Buck's eyes widened. "You think we should go over there and talk to him?"

Before she could join the conversation, Lauralee saw Chief Shank come around the side of the courthouse. He moved toward her but spoke to Deputy Vaughn. "We're needed at Blue Bells," he said in a gruff tone. Without saying hello to anyone, he turned away and crossed the road.

Buck said firmly, "We should talk to Oliver."

"All right," Piper said, stepping out of line.

Lauralee stared at them. "What are you doing? You can't go over there and ask him how he liked being a monkey . . ."

"Buy me a paper?" Piper asked, handing her a coin.

First time first in line, and look at this!

Lauralee followed them. "If I don't get a newspaper, I'm going to take your fancy flower sun hat and beat you with it."

Scared, Piper laughed in delight. She climbed the two steps onto the dais. Buck followed her, and then Lauralee joined them. "Oliver?" Piper called.

Lauralee moved toward the office and peered inside. Tickets had been stacked to one side, and a lunch pouch sat on the stool near the counter. The maroon vest hung on a peg on the wall.

"He's probably on the tracks checking the lines," Piper said, seemingly noticing the vest too, as Lauralee did, and understanding that Oliver was now conducting and not selling tickets.

Suddenly, a chattering noise sounded. Lauralee saw the monkey bolt across the dais and jump into Buck's arms.

Piper stared in their direction. "He's wearing the black vest."

"There's an obvious explanation for this," Lauralee said firmly.

"Yeah, there is," Buck cut in. "Oliver turned into a monkey again."

*   *   *

Lauralee didn't know what to think except that things had turned decidedly odd. If there was one thing she could count on, it was Oliver Beckett acting like the boor he was; he didn't play practical jokes. He wasn't that interesting. What Beckett was, was *on the job*. Efficient. Responsible. He was the high-falutin station agent in Victor City and proud of it.

So where was he? He'd obviously started work because his lunch pouch was on the stool in his office. He couldn't have gone on an errand; no businesses had opened yet. Oliver wasn't in line to buy a newspaper . . .

In fact, neither was Lauralee and the cart had already arrived. Piper saw the cart at the same time and descended the dais steps. Lauralee followed but with more determination in her gait. There was one thing she meant to do today and that was to find Oliver Beckett.

By the time she and Piper crossed the road, the line at the newspaper cart had thinned and Deputy Vaughn handed over his coin for the last paper in the wagon. He nodded to Piper but when he glanced at Lauralee, he smiled wickedly, opened the *Gazette*, and leaned against the courthouse steps' railing to take his leisure in reading it.

She stopped in front of him, intending to report a missing person, but the newspaperman spoke over her. "Did you find out who stole the earrings?"

"What do you know about it?" Vaughn asked without taking his eyes off the printed page.

Felton Ewing shrugged. He reminded Lauralee of a circling shark, with his white-blond hair, ashen face, and cold-blooded nature. The only thing pleasant about him was his love for birds. He imitated their songs on the piccolo that he played in the evenings on his front porch. "I heard one of our town's visitors is missing some jewelry. Perhaps I'm faster on the uptake than our local law boys."

Vaughn replied by turning the page of his newspaper.

"What earrings, Felton?" Lauralee asked, stepping toward the cart.

Newspaper crinkled sharply as Deputy Vaughn pushed off the railing. "It's none of your business."

"It seems we have a thief among us. A cat burglar, that's what they call them in Chicago." Felton didn't look at Deputy Vaughn, but at Lauralee and Piper.

Piper gazed at her. "Cat burglar," she mouthed in awe.

Felton stepped onto the floorboard and sat on the bench seat of the cart. "In the deepest of night, the cat burglar paws his way along the rooftop, slips through an unlocked window, unseen, and robs the occupants while they sleep. The cat carries with him a set of small steel blades that he uses to claw the sleepers' throat if they dare to wake."

Deputy Vaughn now stood next to Lauralee. "Or maybe our visitor *misplaced* her earrings last night and will find them today."

Felton Ewing contemplated the saloon. "I wonder who it is that suddenly has a craving to go out after dark and climb onto the roofs?"

"We could set out milk," Piper said, getting into the spirit of the matter.

"Leave the investigation to the authorities," Vaughn told her gently.

Felton chuckled and smiled at the young women. "Lock your windows tight tonight. You never know when the cat will strike next." He slapped the reins and the cart rolled away.

Lauralee stared at Deputy Vaughn. "Is he telling the truth?"

"No."

She followed him when he turned on his heel and walked toward the bridge. Piper followed Lauralee. She asked, "Is there such a thing as a cat burglar?"

"In big cities, but not in Victor," he said importantly, as if to impress Piper. "And they don't carry blades and claw people. They are thieves, nothing more."

"So who stole the woman's earrings?" Lauralee asked, trying to keep up with him.

He turned on her quickly so that she nearly cannoned into the back of him. "She *misplaced* the earrings. Stay out of this, Lauralee. Don't ask the victim a lot of questions."

"So there is a victim?"

"There is no victim."

"You just said . . ."

His green eyes narrowed on her and his nostrils flared as he took a long breath. "Do you believe everything you hear, Lauralee?" He glanced at Piper, who watched them keenly. He said, "Now you've got Piper believing there's a cat burglar."

Appalled, Lauralee pointed at her friend. "*She* believes Oliver is a monkey."

"So do I," he seethed. Sticking the newspaper beneath his arm, he turned to walk away.

Piper cackled but stopped abruptly when Lauralee narrowed her eyes and said, "Hand me your hat. I owe you a beating."

"Oh, don't take Vaughn seriously. He's ridiculous."

"He shouldn't be allowed to carry a gun." Lauralee fumed and moved toward the boardwalk again. She studied the train depot as they walked. There was still no sign of Beckett.

They stepped onto the next walkway, in front of the saloon, right where Tommy Whitworth and Larry Norris squatted in front of the monkey and stuck a handmade paper hat on top of its head. The monkey didn't seem to mind the new chapeau, probably because it was made with the comic strips, and he eagerly took peanuts from Tommy's outstretched hand.

Piper asked Lauralee, "Do you think there's anything to the cat burglar theory?"

"Obviously there was a crime, since Shank pulled Vaughn out of line to visit Blue Bells," Lauralee told her, walking off the boardwalk, crossing the alley, and climbing onto the walkway in front of Blue Bells Tenement. She stopped midstride and gazed into the road, where Chief Shank stood staring at the second story of the hotel. "What is he staring at?"

Missing the question, Piper grabbed her elbow. "What if it's Levi?" Her tone was hushed now. Her eyes went to the southwest and the foothills there. "What if he comes off the mountain to claw us in our sleep?"

"It's not Levi," Lauralee assured her.

Levi was the only name anyone knew him by. Nobody knew for sure if he was living or a ghost, but someone or something caused the queer lights on the crest of the deserted mining town. It was a sight the citizens of Victor beheld on cold, clear nights. Years before, two deputies had investigated the phenomenon, the gyrating lamps that moved up and down the hillside, but they had never found anything—not even footprints. Then the rumor began: *Levi lives up there forsaken, killing small animals with his bare hands and calling demons with the bones of them.* Some folks thought Big Buck had started the tale, but Lauralee didn't believe it. Buck Lamar was as scared of the lights as everybody else, maybe more so.

"How do you know it's not Levi?" Piper insisted.

"Because there's been no murder. Earrings are missing. What would Levi do with a pair of earrings?" She gazed southward too, but not at the hills—at the grocers. Uncle Todd climbed down the steps carrying a sack of food. Peaches and apples stuck out of the top of the sack.

Piper saw him too and said, "Dr. Thomas is up early; dressed fancy too. Where's he going?"

"I don't know." Lauralee saw that he'd pulled the day buggy in front of the house and put the sack of groceries in the boot of it.

"He bought enough fruit, didn't he?" Piper observed. "Maybe he heard about the monkey and—"

"No," Lauralee interrupted with a smile. "I'll bet he's going to visit the Petrovas." She touched her friend's arm. "I'll see you later, Piper. I'm going with Uncle Todd."

Chapter Five

As the morning wore on, the wind fell and the air grew heavy. Tree-garbed slopes rose from the edge of town. The peak of a high mountain stood sharp and white above the fir trees. To the south, curtains of rain slanted down, and the sky above the mountains was dark with thunderclouds.

They came to a gate. Beyond it, a rutted lane cut through an open field toward a cluster of houses. It wasn't a town, but a community of eight homes beneath a clump of seven trees, and it was known as Wolf Whistle Creek.

Todd halted the carriage in the center drive. He hopped from the footboard and pulled the food sack and his doctor bag from the boot. Lauralee disembarked too, knowing the community's women stared at them from behind their curtains. They might've been ironing or peeling potatoes, but as soon as the buggy arrived, they rushed for their windows.

That's what she would do, anyway.

She glanced out at the fields. Beans grew there, and corn and wheat. Children played outside. Two boys in bib overalls and caps watched the men work in the fields. A mutt sat next to them with its tongue lolling.

"I'll be a small time with the Petrovas," Todd told her, walking toward the Thompsons' old house. It was a large home with a stonework entry and a dark wooden door. Lauralee bid him good-bye and moved toward the Becketts' house with the intention of learning where Oliver Beckett had been disappearing off to and why.

Their home was a simple, one-story cottage with three rooms, as Lauralee recalled. It was whitewashed and stood heartily amid Mrs. Beckett's flower garden. Lauralee saw the woman at the north side of the house, and when she saw Lauralee, Esme smiled and waved.

"Good morning. My uncle is visiting your new neighbors, and I thought I would stop and say hello."

"I'm so happy that you did," Esme Beckett told her. "Come inside."

"Oh, no, I don't want to stop you from gardening. I'll help if you like."

Esme Beckett wore a checkered apron over her black dress. She was a handsome woman in her late fifties. She'd pulled her steel-gray hair into a large bun, and little wisps clung to her neck and cheeks. "I suppose you help your mama garden, don't you? How is Katie?"

"She and Papa will be home on Sunday, and I'll find out. They've been gone thirteen days."

"And you miss them," Esme finished. She held pruning shears in her hand and examined the bush in front of her. "I still miss Matthew." She spoke of her husband, who'd died two years previously.

"I'm glad you decided to stay in Colorado."

"I never seriously considered moving back to Spain. This is my home, my memories are here, and Oliver is here. He has a good job."

It was Lauralee's opening. She asked, "Is Oliver home?" She pulled a spent flower off a buckwheat plant.

"No, dear, of course not. He's at the depot. Didn't you see him?"

"I know he was there this morning, early, but later I couldn't find him."

Esme snipped at a long stem and then put the flower into a basket near the steps. "I'm sure he'll be flattered that you missed him."

"I missed him yesterday too. Did he come home last night?"

Esme's dark eyes found hers. "Yes . . . he was later than usual, but he came home." The crease between her brows deepened. "Why do you ask, Lauralee?"

She let out her breath and grinned at the older woman. "You wouldn't believe me if I told you."

Mrs. Becket smiled but she remained silent, waiting for Lauralee to continue.

"Oh, you know those fool men at Buck's . . . they thought Oliver had been magically turned into a monkey."

"Goodness. They must have been very drunk."

She nodded. "You would think so."

"What made them believe such a thing?"

Lauralee stepped away from the buckwheat plant to explain. "Well, there *is* a monkey in town."

"Really?"

She nodded. "Yes. We think it came in on the train with the gypsy."

"Excuse me?"

Her face drained of color so quickly that Lauralee wondered if Esme had taken sick. She stepped closer and touched Esme's arm.

"Who did you say came in on the train?"

"A gypsy . . ." Lauralee walked with Esme toward the steps. "What's the matter, Mrs. Beckett? Are you ill?"

The woman looked as if she'd had a shock. Perspiration broke out at her hairline. "I can't do it again. I can't do it without Matthew. We have no money. I can't give her any money."

"Sit down, Mrs. Beckett. I'm going to find Uncle Todd."

Esme gripped Lauralee's wrist hard. Her dark eyes searched hers. "No. No, dear, I'm fine."

Confused, she waited. "Mrs. Beckett, do you know the gypsy?"

"Of course not." The woman looked away and got to her feet. "I . . . I need to find Oliver. Where is my shawl?"

"We'll give you a ride to town. As soon as Uncle Todd is finished speaking with your neighbors, we'll take you there."

"All right, dear. All right."

"Would you like me to find your shawl?"

"No, dear. I don't need a shawl," she said, looking as if she wondered why Lauralee mentioned the shawl.

"I thought you said—never mind. We'll wait in the carriage if you like." Once Mrs. Beckett was seated, Lauralee asked, "Who were you talking about giving money to?"

"I don't know what you mean." The woman would no longer look at Lauralee but stared off toward the gates.

"You said you couldn't do it again and that you have no money."

"I meant . . . the garden. I need supplies. I need to tell Oliver about the supplies."

* * *

Esme Beckett barely spoke on the ride into town, though Todd made a noble effort to engage the woman in conversation regarding the weather and such. When he halted the buggy in front of his office, Mrs. Beckett got out without a thank-you and walked toward the depot. She strolled right down the middle of the west road, heedless of buggies and horses.

Todd said in a low voice, "Mighty peculiar acting, isn't she?"

"She's scared," Lauralee said and walked toward the depot behind the woman. It was nearly time to prepare dinner, but she decided to put off the duty until she had seen that Esme got to where she was going safely.

Before she was even with the courthouse, Lauralee saw Oliver Beckett. He was at his usual place on the dais, near the office. His black hair sat curled wildly atop his head, and his dark eyes glinted irritably when he saw his mother climb the depot steps.

Lauralee didn't venture farther. She would've liked to hear what they said, but she could see that they were arguing. Oliver jammed his beefy fists on his hips as Esme spoke ardently to him. Exasperated, he lifted his eyes toward the courthouse.

Quickly, Lauralee pretended she'd dropped something on the boardwalk. She studied the bleached wood and crevices. When she glanced their way again, Esme and Oliver had descended the steps and moved together toward Naberling Creek Bridge.

Lauralee crossed after them. She followed along beyond the department store and the library. When Esme peered behind them, Lauralee skipped into the nearest doorway and entered the police station. She could see the Becketts through the large plate-glass window. They entered Victor City Church.

"What are you doing here?"

Lauralee spun around to see Deputy Vaughn at the desk. When she didn't answer, he asked, "What do you want?"

Well, what did she want? A person didn't just *stop by* a police station. "Er . . . I wondered if I could . . . see your newspaper. I never read it this morning."

"I gave it to Piper."

"Oh, I'll . . . get it from Piper then."

It was in the middle of this enthralling conversation that Reuben Shank walked through the door. He didn't greet Lauralee, didn't even seem to notice her, for that matter, and he skirted around the tall counter. His height and breadth made Deputy Vaughn look like a skinny kid. He barked, "Did you get that wire from San Francisco like I told you?"

"It's on your desk," Vaughn answered, standing sharper now.

"What did it say?"

"He's been hired by Ticktin Law Group." The deputy turned away from the counter and followed Shank toward the back of the room. "He's all clear there."

Shank picked up a telegraph paper from his desk. "What about Creighton?"

"Nothing yet, sir."

Lauralee took her chance to exit the building, feeling grateful that she didn't have to explain further why she'd visited the station in the first place. Vaughn would accuse her of dogging the Becketts and would've thrown her into the hoosegow until she paid a two-dollar fine.

Studying the church, she saw no signs of activity. Perhaps Esme decided to speak to Pastor Carmichael. Walking northward again, Lauralee crossed the bridge and moved toward her uncle's house, with a sense of satisfaction that she'd accomplished what she'd set out to do today, and that was to find Oliver Beckett. She would still like to know where the gypsy was, however, and why the woman had come to Victor City. She might've intended to see Esme, intended to ask for money from the Becketts . . .

It was while Lauralee pondered the question that Big Buck stepped out of the telegraph office and nearly knocked her over. He righted her and started to apologize, but she spoke over him. "Where's the monkey?" She said this on the attack because she wanted a quick, candid answer, with no hesitation.

"Playing dice with Billy Yank. I think the monkey's winning . . ."

"Do you know that Oliver Beckett is over at church right now?"

"I got no problem with that," he told her stiffly, as though he were being questioned in a court of law. "A man's religion is his own business."

She shook her head. "I'm trying to tell you that Oliver is not the monkey."

"Shoot, I know that," Buck answered, relaxed now. "Oliver never could beat Yank at dice, and I assume if he were a monkey he'd be worse at it then he was before his monkeyness."

She paused a moment to understand what he'd just said. Meanwhile, Buck leaned his large frame onto a stonework planter in which ginger-colored cosmos and lavender bluettes reached for the sun. Lauralee leaned there beside him. "What do you know about gypsies, Buck?"

"Much as anybody, I guess. They're a secretive bunch."

She shifted her weight so that she could face him. "Can a gypsy really turn someone into a monkey?"

"I heard tell of some peculiar things when I was a boy. There is a tribe that uses black magic." He dropped his voice so that Lauralee had to lean closer to hear him. "I think they're in cahoots with Lucifer. They use ancient arts to cast spells and turn the evil eye on the unsuspecting. They're called the *Kalderasha*."

"*Kalderasha . . . ,*" she whispered, letting the word wash over her. "What is it?"

He straightened and spoke louder. "A tribe, like I told you." He turned his face toward the south, toward the mountains and the gray skies building dark and thundery. "I feel a bitter breeze when I speak of them."

Lauralee gazed toward the south too, and she sensed an ill will just because he mentioned it, and because the storm grew closer by the moment. Low gray clouds rolled over one another. She shot Buck a nervous glance. "Why are you looking off that way, as if you're talking about Levi?"

"I didn't say nothing about Levi."

"But there's nothing out there except Levi . . . You think he can blow this way with the storm?"

Buck's face took on a wan and worried look. He pushed himself off the planter, edgy, jumpy, and he said, "I gotta go; gotta lock the upstairs before the storm hits."

"Me too," she squeeked out and hurried across the road to Todd's house.

A small balcony jutted off the second floor of Blue Bells. To reach it, Dante had to climb out his window. There wasn't space enough for a chair, so he stood and observed Victor City after nightfall. The saloon was lit, and Dante could hear the piano. It didn't sound too good.

Dante had learned to play the piano at age two. His mother had taught him. After she left, he continued to play—it was his way of keeping her there with him. He envisioned, in his young mind, that she might walk by and hear him play. She would stand there on Nob Hill, and the beautifully played chords would touch her heart. Then she would rush inside the house as she remembered how much she loved her young Dante . . .

It never happened, that foolish yearning of a child.

Lightning cut across the sky to the south. *It will rain tomorrow,* Lauralee had told him. *By God, she was right.* He placed both hands on the railing. *Watch and see,* she'd said.

What was it about the young woman that intrigued him? He knew it was more than her good nature, as he'd first thought. She had a spirit about her that reminded him of something sweet and good.

Thunder rumbled. A strong breeze whipped the courthouse flag. It was a cool wind, and it went through the material of Dante's long-sleeved shirt. He watched the street. Surely the storm would bring Emelina out of her hiding place. She would need to seek a more permanent shelter.

He'd searched everywhere for her, in stores, shops, restaurants, and the stables. The fellow at the train depot had acted oddly when Dante asked if he'd seen a Roma woman, and he never admitted that he had. But he'd acted angry, agitated. What was his name again . . . Oliver?

Dante had a sharp sense that time was running out. Chief Shank acted reserved whenever he spoke to him now. Did the man suspect that he had something to do with the morning burglary? He'd seen Shank staring at his window.

That meant it was time to leave town—and soon. Dante had thought it through, and already he'd purchased a small satchel of food in case he needed to make a quick getaway into the foothills.

A blinding flash rent the sky. In that moment of brightness,

Dante saw someone slip along the walkway in front of the bank. Whoever it was wore a long skirt and a wrap . . . He pushed himself off the railing. Emelina!

Thunder woke her. The storm that had been building all day was nearly upon them. Lauralee sat in bed and swung her feet to the floor. She could smell the rain through the partly opened window.

She stood to shut the curtain and saw that no rain had fallen. Only the smell of it was on the stiff breeze that whipped the courthouse flag. Here on the top floor of the house, she had a good view of the north side of town. The street lamp threw light into the train depot. Across the alley, gas-lantern light streamed through the saloon windows and beneath the doors. Two horses stood tethered to the snorting post, and they pranced nervously when thunder rolled again. A man stepped out of the saloon and took their reins.

Lauralee lifted her hand to pull the drapery closed, but when lightning brightened the walkway in front of the telegraph office, she saw that someone stood there. She leaned forward, straining to see who it was.

A bell tinkled.

The monkey bolted out from beneath the barroom doors, scampered across the roadway, and jumped into the outstretched arms of whoever stood in front of the telegraph office.

It was the gypsy. Lauralee was sure of it.

She raced toward the chair in the corner of the room and found her trumpet skirt. Slipping into it, she raced downstairs while buttoning her blouse. She took her rain slicker from the coat rack, draped it over her shoulders, and quietly stepped onto the porch. Lauralee gazed at her feet. She'd forgotten her boots!

Not wanting to take the time to fetch them, she descended the steps and slipped through the gate barefooted. Shutters rattled. A door slammed. The wind seized her slicker and tried to rip it out of her hands, but Lauralee held it tightly and wrapped it around her shoulders and hair. She crossed the street and stepped onto the boardwalk in front of the undertaker's office.

This was right about the time that caution caught up to her. She'd underestimated the eeriness of the storm and the darkness of the shadows. Stealing along the walkway, she came to the gap between buildings. Fear pawed at her. Didn't a black alley make a convenient passageway for a cat burglar on his way to work? Lauralee could almost hear the short blades spring forth from the burglar's hands, feel them slashing at her in the darkness.

Lightning flashed, giving her a quick view of the alley. There was nothing there but a garbage bin. Darkness returned. Lauralee streaked across the silent, creepy blackness until at last she stood in front of the bank. Awnings knocked and rattled with the gusting wind . . . and then a pair of strong hands grabbed her shoulders. "Hello, Emelina," a deep voice said.

Chapter Six

Lauralee screamed wildly, or started to, but a hand covered her mouth. Someone pushed her against the bank wall and pulled the slicker off her head. "Lauralee?"

She stopped struggling to stare at her attacker, barely making out the outline of his face and thick hair.

"It's me, Dante Quinn." He dropped his hand from her mouth.

Lauralee shoved him on the chest. "You horrible man. Why did you grab me like that?"

"I thought you were someone else," he mumbled peevishly, taking a step away from her and glancing up and down the road. He wore a dark shirt and trousers, as though he meant to keep himself hardly visible. Looking at her again, he asked, "What are you doing out here?"

"Well . . ."

What was she doing out here? Surely Quinn would call her rash if she shared the reason she'd bolted outside barefooted.

"Er . . . taking a walk."

"Of course," he said blandly. "What better time to stroll than during a lightning storm."

"All right. I thought I saw your gypsy from my window . . ."

"Where?" he asked, leaning closer.

"In front of the telegraph office."

He jerked his head in that direction. Palest light touched his features, and Lauralee could see a hard glint in his eyes. "Go back inside," he told her, turning northward. He stepped toward the telegraph office by way of the sawmill, moving swiftly, lithely.

Lauralee kept up with him. She remained quiet when he studied the lumber pile in the middle of the yard. Lightning lit the area, revealing nothing untoward. A large drop fell on her slicker, and Lauralee covered her head again. She moved when Dante moved, paused when Dante paused. He climbed onto the boardwalk. So did she. When they stood beneath the telegraph office easement, hard rain began to fall. Giant drops hit the gravel road. Lauralee stood behind Dante, letting him shield her from the blowing rain. She told him, "I could've sworn she would still be here." She felt the need to shout this because of the pounding rain.

Mr. Quinn vaulted straight up three feet.

"Don't tell me you didn't know I was behind you?" she asked.

Spinning around, he wore a dark scowl. "What are you trying to do, scare me to death?"

"Yes," she bantered. She couldn't help it; a smile spread across her lips. "That's exactly what I was trying to do."

With a snarl, he bounded into the rain and jogged toward the courthouse. He got quite wet as he stopped to stare left and right, and then he trotted around the last building on the road and out of sight.

Lauralee still laughed, but she stopped and cleared her throat as she realized she stood alone again on the deserted road. Rain blew across the gravel in sheets. Lightning jagged above the telegraph office. Lauralee ran toward Marigold's as the thunder cracked overhead. Skirting the wall, she ran for the covered walkway at the courthouse opposite the train depot.

Now where had Dante Quinn disappeared to? She was sure he'd found his way to the station. She leaned forward to see if he was at the top of the steps and then leaned back when lightning struck again.

She hadn't heard the old woman's approach, but when Lauralee turned around, the gypsy stood there. "Oh my goose," Lauralee proclaimed, grabbing her heart. "Where did you come from?" Shouldn't there have been some warning, like a puff of smoke or a hail of toads?

In the depot's lamplight, gray eyes studied Lauralee unhurriedly. Then, with a thick accent, the old woman explained, "You have *kpache*."

"Excuse me?"

The gypsy stepped closer. "You have much *kpache*." Her silver hair fell to her waist, and misty droplets clung to the roots near her forehead. She wore a dingy-colored blouse that fell loosely on her shoulders.

"What is *kpache?*"

"A sense of things, *va?* Your mind is open to see the unseen and to hear the voices in the next sphere."

"Oh," Lauralee said, impressed.

"Do you hear the voices of your mind?"

"Songs mostly. Over and over sometimes. It took me three days to get 'Oh My Darling Clementine' out of my head."

"There are voices tonight," the woman said spookily. "All around us."

Lauralee stood with her back against the bricks. "Wonderful." And she didn't mean it in a cheery way.

The gypsy wasn't looking at her now, but at the clouds.

When she'd lifted her chin, Lauralee saw a stone on a chain around the woman's neck. It was dark and beautiful, but it also reminded her of a drop of blood. "What is that, a ruby?" Lauralee asked her, stepping forward.

Gray eyes found hers again and she touched the necklace. "It is a powerful amulet. It watches over me, *va?* It holds spells and enchantments." She turned as if she meant to walk out into the rain.

Lauralee thought to delay the woman, hoping Dante Quinn would find his way back to the courthouse. "Will you read my palm?" she asked quickly.

"It is my greatest skill," the woman said, turning around again.

Lauralee held out her hand.

"It is empty."

"Is that bad?"

Smiling tolerantly, the gypsy advised, "It should have money in it."

Lauralee dug into the pocket of her skirt. "I only have a quarter."

The woman snatched it from her as quickly as the lightning crossed the sky. Gripping Lauralee's wrist with surprising strength, she said, "You have thick hands."

"I beg your pardon?"

"It is good to have thick hands, child. It means you are healthy and your nature is joyful." She twisted Lauralee's palm toward the lamplight. "Fire hands. In this I must caution you. You are likely to have accidents."

"I am rather prone . . ."

"Your heart line is strong." She touched Lauralee's hand with her crooked finger. "There is romance in your future."

"Really?" Lauralee asked, studying her palm as well.

"But you must pass love's test."

"Test?" she asked, wrinkling her brow. "What sort of test?"

"For fifty cents I could see more."

"I'm out of money."

The old woman stroked her palm. "You have a break in your union line."

That didn't sound good. "What does that mean?"

"A relationship will end."

Lauralee stared at her hand. "The romance?"

"The union line is not for romance. It is a family line. The break will be with your father, or brother, or some other male member of your household."

Lauralee pulled her hand away from the gypsy's. "That is not possible."

The old woman cackled. The sound of it was throaty, coarse, and it mingled with the rumble of thunder overhead. "Would you like to read mine?"

"I don't know how to do it."

"You have *kpache*. I know it. I feel it."

Lauralee took the old woman's hand gingerly. "All right. Er . . ." She considered the palm thrust beneath her nose. It was deeply cut with jagged seams, some feathered into chainlike ridges. Other grooves were curved and cracked. The old woman's hand was like the wrinkled map Lauralee had seen in the telegraph office.

Nothing came to her. If Lauralee had *kpache,* shouldn't she see something? Shouldn't she be able to see why the gypsy ran from Dante Quinn or where she hid from him? "I see . . . fear."

The gypsy cackled. "Try again, *va?*"

"All right." She shifted her weight. What had Big Buck told her? *"Kalderasha."*

The woman's brow raised and her eyes met Lauralee's "Very good. Do you know the *Kalderasha?*"

"Me? Heck no." She saw the gypsy frown and changed her tone. "Sorry. I meant no offense." Taking the woman's hand again, she continued. "You've come to see someone. A woman."

"You disappoint me."

"Er . . . someone is coming to see you . . . following you," Lauralee told her in a rush, trying to keep the conversation going.

The gypsy's eyes darkened. "The man who follows me will die tonight." She pulled her hand away from Lauralee's. In the lamplight her features stiffened and a sneer curled over her crooked teeth. "Run home. Go quickly."

Lauralee pushed herself off the wall.

The look in the woman's eyes had turned malevolent as she stared toward the train station. Dante Quinn stood on the platform, staring eastward toward the Naberling Creek Bridge.

"Baxt!" the gypsy spit out. When Lauralee gazed at her again, the old woman stared at the sky and the rolling black clouds there. She mumbled indistinguishable words and lifted her hands to the sky.

Lauralee backed away as the lightning flashed brighter. Thunder rolled through the valley, tripling its force. The wind raged from the south. Across the road, men watched the storm from the saloon doors. She stared at the gypsy a last time. The old woman had lifted her hands toward the sky.

Lauralee turned and ran from the covered walkway, sensing a spiteful spirit on her heels. Rain pounded her slicker. She splashed in the gravel and mud in her bare feet. Ahead of her, she saw Dante Quinn step off the dais to meet her. She screamed above the noise: "Come inside with me. You're not safe out here."

"No, she's close. I know it. She's got to be here."

"Yes, she is."

Dante reached out and took Lauralee by the shoulders. He pulled her face close to his. "You saw her? Where?"

"The courthouse. But don't go there. Come inside with me."

Dante released her and took several steps toward the building. Lauralee watched him for a moment and then heard an unremitting rumbling sound behind her. In the blackness she could barely make out the twisting cloud on the ground. All she could see was greenish-white rolling shapes directly behind the saloon. *"Tornado!"* she screamed. She ran for cover but was too slow. The bottom of her skirt lifted as the funnel wobbled north and east. Her slicker coat was ripped from her grasp.

A pair of arms went around her, pulling her roughly toward the building. Lauralee skid through the gravel on her knees as Dante dragged her into the covered doorway. He huddled over her, and Lauralee closed her eyes.

It sounded as if the train had jumped the tracks and hit a building. The street lamp exploded. Wood cracked and splintered. Rocks flew halfway down the west road.

And then it was over. Dante turned and glanced into the street. Lauralee peered beyond his shoulder and saw the rain came in sheets. Lightning flashed, thunder boomed, and small hail pellets dropped from the sky.

"Are you all right?"

"I think so." She tried to catch her breath. When Dante moved toward the street, Lauralee grabbed his arm. "Don't go."

"You're fine. Stay beneath the shelter."

"But you're not safe. She said you would die tonight."

She couldn't see his face but knew that he hesitated. "You spoke to her?"

"Yes . . . she was right here . . . No, Dante, don't go."

"Lauralee, let loose of my arm."

"She said you would die and she called the tornado . . . *She called it!*"

"Stop it, Lauralee. She did no such thing." And then he ran into the rain. She could see only his outline as he ducked and weaved. He moved across the road and toward the south.

Others ventured outside. Lauralee saw the newspaperman, Felton Ewing, standing on the walkway and staring at the train station. He watched Dante cross the road, and then he too ran into the rain, but northward, like the others who'd come outside.

Men carrying torches raced for the train depot. It seemed the storm's only casualty except for bits of roofing off the saloon. The twister had scattered wood pieces all across the road, and even a portion of the tracks had been lifted. Todd was among the men who studied the damage. With no casualties discovered, the men returned indoors.

The rain abated little when Dante Quinn found Lauralee again. "She's gone." They stood in the road in front of Blue Bells. "What did she say to you?"

Lauralee raised her palms. "That I have thick hands . . ."

"What?" His hair dripped rainwater down the sides of his face. In the torchlight, he appeared more determined than she'd ever seen him.

"She read my palm. And then I read hers." When he narrowed his eyes, she said hurriedly, "I was trying to guess where she was staying, trying to find out some information for you, but all she said was that tonight, the man who searched for her would die. She started mumbling something and the storm worsened."

They stood alone now, as most people had moved off. Uncle Todd already stood on his porch and opened the door. Dante gazed at Lauralee again. "You don't really believe that."

"It's not a matter of whether I believe it or not. I know what happened. I saw it."

He sighed and released her. "You're a very gullible person; do you know that?"

"I was helping *you*."

"I didn't ask for your help." He spun away from her and walked toward the porch.

Angry now, she groused, "You are the most distrustful man I've ever known."

"I want you to stay out of this, Lauralee," he said, opening the screen. "I will find her by myself from now on."

"There's more to this than a court case, isn't there? This is personal. Who is she, Dante? And don't say Emelina Istok, because that's not enough."

"I don't owe you anything," he meted out, stepping toward her again. "I don't even know you, and you expect me to tell you my personal matters. This is my concern." Leaning in, he nailed the last of it. "If I were going to trust anyone to help me, it certainly wouldn't be a woman like you. I'd ask Shank or one of his men."

Frustrated, Lauralee remained in the middle of the gravel road, in the rain, and watched Dante hop onto the walk in front of the tenement house. The next moment he stepped inside and was gone from view. He was an awful man. Horrible. And she was glad indeed that he didn't want her help—because she would never offer it again.

Despite the fact that Lauralee would turn twenty-one in August, Rick seemed to think he needed to escort her home on Sunday morning. She'd bought the supplies he'd requested earlier in the week, and it was a good thing too, since most of the men in town, including the grocer, were clearing debris at the train station. Logs were being hauled to the sawmill, and the rails were being cleared. Rick watched their progress as he packed the supplies and Lauralee's trunk onto buckboard.

"Give your mama a kiss from me," Todd called to Lauralee from the porch.

"I'm sure she'll come to town soon." She stood at the gate and waved to her cousin Daniel, who was already awake and watching the men work. He and his friends dangled their feet on the boardwalk and off railings in front of Marigold's Kitchen.

She glanced toward Blue Bells and wondered if Dante Quinn was awake yet. There was no sign of him anywhere, but Lauralee noticed that Reuben Shank stepped off the boardwalk and moved toward the boardinghouse instead of helping with the work. His gait had determination to it. Deputy Vaughn and another man, Deputy Casillo, followed Shank, and Lauralee wondered if there'd been another burglary.

Rick touched her elbow and led Lauralee to the passenger seat. He climbed aboard himself and flicked the reins.

Dante, already dressed and with hat in hand, saw Reuben Shank through the window. He walked straight toward Blue Bells, with two deputies behind him.

That meant it was time to go.

Setting his hat on his head, he turned to open the door while stuffing the pearl necklace into his jacket pocket. A single bulb burned in the hallway. Dante stepped left and twisted the knob to the back door that led to the stairwell.

It wouldn't turn.

He shook the handle again but stopped when he heard footfalls on the main stairway.

Chapter Seven

Think," Dante told himself. He moved left and tried the door directly across from his room. It opened noiselessly, and he slipped inside the room, locking the door behind him.

Darkness greeted him. Someone had drawn all the shades . . . and that someone breathed heavily from somewhere in the middle of the room. Dante couldn't remember if he'd seen who'd rented this, and he hoped it wasn't Roy Bean or Wyatt Earp.

The tremendous snore that ripped through the space did little to calm his nerves. He stood stock-still and waited. When soft breathing sounded again, Dante tiptoed toward the window and snaked his hand behind the shade. He pulled the pin from the lock on top of the window.

Across the hall, knuckles hit a door. "Open up, Quinn," Shank demanded.

Dante shoved on the window frame, and the glass slid upward. Shank pounded harder on the other door. Someone else spoke; Dante recognized the desk clerk's voice. "I've got the key. You don't have to break it down."

He lifted his leg and had it out the window when the soft breathing ceased. The figure on the bed sat straight up and a woman's voice screamed, "Cat burglar . . . *it's the cat burglar!*"

He practically fell out the window in his haste but caught himself on the small balcony's railing. The narrow terrace to his left offered an iron stairway, a fire escape, and the only way to reach it was to jump the distance between the two landings. Dante climbed onto the first railing and balanced himself using a gable above his head.

From inside the room he heard the chief hollering to the woman to open the door. The desk clerk had apparently run downstairs for another key. Dante furrowed his brow in concentration. There was perhaps nine feet between the railings.

The chief pounded another round of knocking, and Dante heard the bedsprings squeak as the woman got out of bed.

Lamont's car was directly beneath the second window. If he could get to the railing, Dante would drop onto the car. That was the plan. Despite his precarious position, he executed a successful liftoff, sailed the expanse, and missed the railing by a fingertip. He threw out his other hand and caught hold. Gripping the spindle single-handedly, Dante dangled over the Packard for a moment. He took a breath, ready to release the railing, just as one of the deputies rounded the building. Struggling upward, Dante got his shoe on the balcony and then hauled himself over the edge of it.

"Hey," the deputy called to him. "Hey, you. Stop immediately."

On his knees, Dante tried the window, and much to his nervous surprise, the glass slid upward. He dove inside the room just as the deputy stepped onto the fire escape.

Jamming the pin into the window lock, Dante took a cursory glance around the room: The bed was made; the room was quiet; an oil lamp flickered on the desk. But on the chair, near the bed, someone had laid out a large blue dress. On top of the clothing was a fancy bonnet and gloves.

He stepped forward, hearing splashing noises. A woman obviously was freshening herself in the lavatory, which meant she could emerge from the connected room at any moment and was probably naked as a native. Dante gazed at the window again.

The deputy, a skinny man with black hair, pounded on the glass. He glanced left and hollered, "He's in here, Chief. You've got the wrong one."

Dante could hear Shank's footfalls in the next room and his "Take it easy, Lady. You're not hurt." In the hall again, the chief pounded on the door in front of Dante. He hollered at the desk clerk, "This time bring all the keys, Martin, or I'll kick down every door in this hotel." His fist hit the door again.

Trapped, Dante backed toward the window again. There was no way out. Unless . . .

Pulling the blind and ignoring the shouts of the deputy, Dante removed his own hat and threw it on the floor near the lavatory. He shrugged out of his jacket, wadded it, and stuffed it beneath the bed. Slipping the dress over his head, he grabbed the bonnet and tried to remember that he'd once had dignity.

A key turned the lock.

Dante blew out the lamp.

The door opened.

"He's in there—he's in there!" Dante squealed, trying to hit the highest note in his octave range.

Shank wasted no time. He pulled the pistol from his holster and kicked open the lavatory door.

Dante slipped out of the room when Shank stepped in on the woman. The shriek she let out could've peeled the carpet right off the stairway. It started at a high, nerve-freezing pitch and went up from there.

Sliding out the front door and onto the boardwalk, Dante raced around the north side of the building. There he yanked the dress off over his head, removing the hat along with it. He tossed it into the alley and then studied the train depot. Most of the town's people were there, clearing the tornado debris, and all of them stared at Blue Bells Tenement. More than a few men stopped what they were doing and trotted toward the hotel. None of them seemed to notice Dante. He crossed the road leisurely and then jogged over the bridge.

Where to go, where to go . . .

He ran southward, passed the police station, and raced up-hill toward the church. What stood at the back of the building was the answer to Dante's dilemma: a horse, a fine horse, saddled and ready to go.

Mounting the animal, he pulled the reins off the wooden post and kicked the sides of the horse. Just as he pushed the steed toward the trees and the river, he heard someone call out from behind him. "Horse thief!"

Turning in the saddle, Dante saw the fellow he'd met at the train depot, Oliver something or other, standing at the back door to the church. But Oliver didn't cry out again. Looking left and right, he rushed back into the church.

"H'yah!" Dante urged, pushing the horse toward the shal-low river. Branches slapped him. A thorn bush snagged his right leg and ripped a hole in his trousers. Once in the river, he pushed the horse southward. When he saw a path, he urged

the horse into a gallop toward the foothills. Dante slowed when the trail rounded a wooded plat. A buckboard rolled slowly in front of him.

It was a fine and crisp day. They traveled west along the plat, where purple clover bloomed, as did wood lily, pink fireweed, and blueberry willow. Rick directed the buckboard southward, and the majestic peaks of the Rockies loomed ahead. Lauralee gazed at them while feeling the breeze coming off the snowcaps. Suddenly, she heard a horse and rider come alongside the buggy on her brother's left.

"Howdy," Rick greeted, pushing the Stetson off his brow.

Dante Quinn nodded his dark head. Lauralee thought he was dressed oddly to go horseback riding, in his starched white shirt and . . . ripped trousers? When he caught her curious stare, he greeted her. "Miss Murphy." His formal tone suggested that he was still irritated after their argument last night.

"What are you doing out here?" she asked suspiciously, watching him.

He didn't look at her. "Enjoying a ride."

She frowned and then realized that Rick was staring at her. "Sorry. Mr. Quinn. This is my brother, Rick Murphy; Rick, Mr. Dante Quinn."

Rick nodded and seemed unaware of the tension between Lauralee and the man. "Where you headed?"

"I think I'll make my way toward Denver."

"Well, that's the only place you'll wind up heading this way, unless you're stopping by Long Winter Ranch. You're welcome to do that, especially since you're friends with my sister."

Quinn's dark eyes held Lauralee's. "I don't know if you'd

call us friends. We met in your uncle's office when I stopped to see the doctor."

"And she snooped in your business, is that it?" Rick asked without looking at her.

"I did not *snoop*."

Rick chuckled as Quinn's eyes twinkled mischievously.

Lauralee used a crisp tone. "I was merely being friendly. It's my duty, after all, to welcome visitors to town, especially now that Papa will be governor. I was practicing my graciousness."

"You're nosy," Rick told her, and Dante Quinn nodded in agreement.

She eyed them both with malice. "I'm gracious."

Nothing. They ignored her.

Rick spoke to Quinn. "You're still welcome at our home any time."

Dante nodded and then rode ahead of them. After a while he pushed the horse eastward, toward the foothills. Rick didn't comment, but Lauralee knew exactly where Dante Quinn was headed. He meant to ride toward Fool's Peak, the old mining camp. But why? Last night Emelina Istok had been in Victor City. Did he find evidence that the old gypsy had headed that way for some reason? The only way to find out was to ride that direction herself later in the day.

Rick directed the buggy around the circular drive toward the side of the house. Lauralee stepped off the footboard just as her father walked out of the long barn. He wore beige pants and a brown shirt that had bits of hay sticking to it. "Lauralee."

She stepped off the footboard right into her father's arms, never minding the hay. She loved him more than she loved any man in the world.

And what an odd time to think of Dante Quinn.

Dante Quinn was nothing like her father. Yet Lauralee wondered if he was just a little . . . No. Wade Murphy was a brilliant man and a quick study of human character. Dante Quinn might be brilliant, but he was no quick study, or he would've trusted Lauralee when he first met her. Her father was kind and patient. Dante Quinn showed no such attributes.

After her father set her on her feet, she kept her arms around his waist. Wade Murphy was still handsome, though his dark hair had plenty of gray in it. Still lean, he was solid, immovable. Embracing him was like hugging a steel post, except with skin on it. Lauralee frowned at him, remembering something. "Papa, the most important thing in the world to me is your answer to this question."

"It's sad you've never joined the theater. You would've been good at it."

"Are you going to sell the ranch if you become governor?"

His brows drew together over his gray-blue eyes. "Of course not. Whatever gave you that idea?"

She fell into his arms again. "Judge Mitchell said you would sell and move to Denver."

"Well, of course your mother and I would move there if I win." When she pulled away from him, he said, "Oh, come on, Lauralee. You know I can't act as governor on the ranch. I would have to have a home in Denver during session. Don't tell me you've never thought about that."

She dropped her arms to her sides. "I guess I haven't."

"And you can choose whichever place you'd like to live. Rick will run the ranch. You can stay here or live with us in Denver." He kept one arm around her, looking troubled by her questions.

She brightened purposely, for her father's sake. "Well, of course you'll live in Denver, and I will travel back and forth."

"Half the time there and half the time here," he reiterated, looking somewhat relieved. "Yes."

He hugged her closer. "I'm sorry, sweetheart. We really never discussed it, did we? But listen, I may not win the governorship, and all this will be for naught."

"Of course you'll win."

"You never know."

"Where's Mom?" she asked, pulling out of his embrace. "I can't wait to see her."

"She was headed toward the garden the last I saw her." Stepping forward, he began to unload the supplies with Rick.

Lauralee walked around the side of the two-story house, thinking about what her father had said. She didn't like that life changed—and it would change, because her father would certainly win the governor's seat. That meant her parents would be gone for long periods of time, and that saddened her.

Still, she was an adult now. She could handle the situation. And she wanted her mother.

Cutting through the endive, she stalked Katie Murphy through the sunflower patch, and when Katie bent to pull a weed Lauralee poked her head through the leaves.

Katie Murphy jumped a foot. "Don't you know how old I am, Lauralee? My heart could stop beating over a trick like that. Then where would you be? At my grave, that's where, crying for your mama."

Lauralee laughed and stepped through the flowers to embrace Katie. She was still a beautiful woman, though she was full-figured now. Short, she reminded Lauralee of a little apple. She had rosy red cheeks and blond hair, and her pale blue eyes were the same color as the sky. Lauralee asked her, "Did you like Denver?"

"I've been there before," she said when Lauralee released

her. "It's full of crime." She bent again to pull a wildflower from the endive.

Lauralee crouched down beside her mother and asked the question that was most on her mind since she'd compared her father to Dante Quinn. "Was Papa always like he is now? I mean, even though you two started off badly, could you see that he was *the one* man for you when you met him?"

"Good heavens, no."

Lauralee gasped in high drama and stared at her mother. "What are you saying?"

"I was attracted to him, but he was an awful man."

"But he was a brilliant sheriff."

Katie yanked hard on a root that stubbornly held onto the earth. "He thought he was. He thought he knew everything by his gut instinct. Wade Murphy became a better man when he learned he could be wrong about something." The root gave way and Katie nearly fell backward pulling it out of the ground.

"But you saw his kindness and patience, right?"

"I suppose he had a seed of it in him, but I didn't see it when I first met him." She stood and moved along the plants again.

Lauralee followed her. "But he's so loving. How can you say that?"

"I learned all those things later, and maybe I recognized them a little at the time, but the situation we found ourselves in didn't ring with romance. Later, when some of the worst of it was over, I realized I'd fallen in love. But I didn't sit in the jail cell daydreaming over Wade Murphy. I wanted to hit him on the head with something."

Lauralee knew her world would never be the same again. "Well, where's the romance in that?"

Laughing, Katie took Lauralee's arm. "I think those were the most romantic days of my life, sparring with and hating your papa."

"That's outlandish. I don't believe it. I won't believe it."

"That's because you've never been in love."

Lauralee looked out over the yard and toward the barn, where her father still stood at the buckboard talking to Rick. Her father's head bobbed up, and he turned around toward the drive. Rick turned too. Lauralee saw why they stared. A day buggy had pulled into the yard. "Oh, no," she told her mother. "It's Judge Mitchell."

"What do you mean 'oh, no'? I thought you loved that old man."

"I love him, sure, but I've discovered his bigotry. And he's loud. Do you know he's against women's suffrage?"

Still linked arm and arm with Lauralee, she walked toward the barn. "Of course he's against women's suffrage, dear. He's a man."

"Good day, Wade Murphy, good day," the judge shouted as he backed out of the day carriage that he'd parked in the yard. Since he was portly, it took him a long time to get down. Lauralee stopped to feel sorry for the bailiff who, no doubt, had to squish the old man in from behind.

Her father caught Mitchell's arm when he had, at last, two feet on the ground. "Hello, Calvin. What have you been up to?" Wade Murphy was one of the few people who addressed the judge by his first name. They'd been friends since the days when Mitchell was a circuit judge and her father was the sheriff of Victor City.

"Locking up the evil among us," Mitchell answered in his

booming voice. He grinned at Rick and removed his hat when he saw Lauralee and her mother. "My, it's good to be among the kindly."

"Where's Winifred?" Katie asked, speaking of Mitchell's wife.

He held the ear horn to his head. "In town, consoling her sister." When he said it, Katie remembered watching the judge help his wife from a buggy in front of Blue Bells Tenement. Her sister must have been the woman she'd seen with them. Mitchell said, "She woke up with a man in her room."

"That she didn't know?" Rick asked, standing behind their father.

"Too right she didn't know him, the old maid."

Lauralee's mother swatted Rick on the arm. "Mind your manners."

"*My* manners?" Rick asked with his brows arching toward his dark hair. "He called her an old maid."

Katie ignored that and asked the judge, "Did they catch whoever it was?"

"No, he's on the run and Althea, Winnie's sister, is already shook up. I'm afraid she's got a bad opinion of our town. Earlier this week someone stole her earrings."

Lauralee stepped forward. "The cat burglar?"

"Will you stay for lunch and tell us all about it?" Katie asked from behind Lauralee.

"Oh, I don't want to be a bother."

And that was his typical response, because that was the usual reason Judge Mitchell came to Long Winter Ranch— to have lunch or dinner, or even breakfast if the hour was right.

"You're never a bother," Katie assured him, and she led the way into the house.

The Murphy house was built in 1881, beginning as a one-story dwelling made of wood and logs. In 1884, Wade Murphy enlarged the house by adding walls north, east, and south of the original structure. A toilet room was added, making the Murphy family the first in Morgan County to have such a convenience. In 1897, with help from local artisans, a second floor was built and a wide verandah was added to it. The Murphys' friend, Barney Crowe, had filled the rooms of the house with furniture pieces he'd designed and built himself, including the vast pine table with twelve chairs. The five of them now sat at one end of it.

Lauralee wanted Mitchell to mention the cat burglar again, but the judge was intent on finding out about her father's trip to Denver. Finally, the judge said, "Has Lauralee told you what happened in town this week?"

"The twister," Rick said, nodding, and finishing his mouthful. "A twister hit the train depot. Half of it's missing."

"Devil wind," Mitchell agreed. "But I'm talking about the burglaries."

"The cat burglar," Lauralee coaxed.

"That's what that fool Ewing calls him, but I have another name . . . Dante Quinn."

Lauralee dropped her fork.

Rick stared at her. "Your friend we met on the road home? Well, doesn't that just beat all?"

Everyone paused from eating to stare at Lauralee. She defended, "Dante Quinn cannot be the cat burglar."

"Shank thinks it's him," the judge thundered. "Felton

Ewing saw Quinn right after the tornado struck and said Quinn was running in the opposite direction than everyone else. That's about the time the burglary took place too."

"That's because he was looking for the gypsy."

"Gypsy?" came the general question around the table. "What gypsy?"

Rick grumbled, "You're not still going on about that?"

"Quinn is not the cat burglar. He can't be."

"Why can't he be?" her father asked, dropping his napkin into his lap.

Rick answered for her. "Because he's young and handsome."

"I've talked to him. He's no cat burglar." She eyed Rick. "Did you think he was a criminal?"

"I talked to him only once."

"He's a lawyer," she told her father.

"That's enough to convict him right there," the judge added.

Lauralee sat back in her chair. "Well, I don't believe it. I can't. He's not the type."

"Althea got a good look at him in her bedroom. He's a tall, good-looking fellow with dark hair," the judge told her. "I met Quinn only once, but that describes him."

"He's long gone anyway," Rick interjected. "He was riding off to Denver when we saw him this morning."

Lauralee didn't say she'd seen Quinn turn away from the trail. She didn't believe for one moment that Dante Quinn was guilty of thieving. He just wasn't the sort. Quinn upheld the law. Why would he steal? She finished her dinner in silence while the rest of the family and the judge talked about all manner of subjects.

She had to warn him. Before he headed back into Victor

City, Dante Quinn needed to know that Shank was out to arrest him.

Dante watched the rider from his high place in the rocks. He knew Shank would come for him, but it surprised him that the chief came alone.

It was early morning. The night had turned cold in these barren rocks, but it wasn't lonely. Something lived in the foothills near the abandoned mining camp. Dante had heard it during the night. Perhaps it was a black bear; the footfalls had sounded heavy, and there had been growling noises too.

Time passed. Dante rubbed his chin, feeling the grizzle. He hadn't been able to shave. His white shirt was coated with yellow dust, and his hair felt gritty. Tonight he would ride to Victor City again and try to spot Emelina. Dante didn't know what else to do. He was a wanted man. He'd lost his job by now, because his face would be on every handbill across nearby counties. Dante Quinn had become the very thing he'd despised: a drifter, a tramp . . . a gypsy.

Emelina must remove the curse. Personal reasons aside, Dante had to find her. Once she removed the curse, he would turn himself over to Shank and pay what everyone else believed was his debt to society. He figured several years behind bars in a state penitentiary would do it, and he could survive that. Once that was over, Dante hoped he could make a living on a farm or in the mines.

A jackrabbit bounded through the wild grass. It brought Dante's focus to the rider again, who drew closer and then dismounted. It wasn't Shank. The rider was slender—and feminine. Dante could see her pale-colored split skirt, jacket, and black boots.

He switched positions to see her face.

She removed her hat and held it up to block the sun as her eyes surveyed the rocks. Blond hair tumbled to her shoulders . . . Lauralee Murphy.

Dante ducked when she gazed his direction. By God, he should've expected this. As soon as she found out he was a fugitive, she would start searching for him. She would love the mystery and adventure of it all. He peered over the rocks again. Perhaps he should garner her help.

He needed help.

But not from her, not again. He'd learned something the evening he'd had dinner with Lauralee: She could destroy him. Divine, intelligent, bold, and adventurous, the beautiful Miss Murphy was the one woman Dante could never trust, because she would break him just as his mother had broken Nolan Quinn.

The horse snorted, and Dante glanced again to where Lauralee stood. The animal snorted once more and stamped its hooves. Lauralee no longer stared at the rocks, but at the horse. She grabbed the reins.

The animal reared.

Dante pushed himself off the boulder and stood as a rattling noise sounded. He saw Lauralee's reaction. She spun to her left and stared at the ground while backing toward the rocks.

He jumped from his spot between the two boulders and landed in gravel. Picking up a sizable rock, he ran forward to save her.

The horse let out a hysterical cry and ran from Lauralee. She jerked her head around to watch it run, not realizing something moved toward her from the trees to her right.

Dante skidded in the gravel as he beheld the sight: A man circled Lauralee—a giant of a man with tangled hair that hung down his back. He wore torn pants and a stained undershirt.

The diamondback rattled a new warning.

The wild man leaned sideways and snatched up the rattler by the jaws and then swung it like a ribbon over his head.

Lauralee screamed.

The man stepped toward her, jabbed the snake's head at her, and then roared with laughter when she fell against the rock wall.

Dante ran forward again, trying to shove down the panic gripping his chest. When he was near enough, he threw the rock he'd meant to toss at the snake. It hit the wild man between the shoulders.

The man arched with the blow and dropped the snake. The rattler slithered downhill toward the underbrush as the wild man turned to face Dante. *Hideous* described his scarred features. Blisters covered his mouth. His hair shot every direction, and it was matted with lint and dirt. He wore the expression of a man who'd met Satan and admired him. He lunged at Dante.

Dante dropped into the dirt and rolled. Jumping up, he grabbed Lauralee's arm and dragged her behind him. She ran with him but stiff-legged. With all his strength he pulled her into the rocks.

The wild man came after them. He wasn't so fast on foot, but his hands were quick. He caught Dante by the shirt.

Dante turned on him, dealing him a fist in the stomach.

The man didn't flinch, and he backhanded Dante across the temple.

In the dirt, Dante scrambled to escape when the wild man grabbed for him again. Rocks flew overhead. Lauralee had thrown them from her spot near the boulder. The wild man faced her and got ready to charge her, but Dante kicked his legs out from beneath him. The man tumbled and rolled in the gravel.

Springing to his feet, Dante grabbed Lauralee's wrist. This time she ran fast alongside him. They ran downhill, swung right toward the trees, and kept running until they saw Lauralee's horse standing where the ground leveled out. Spooked, the animal danced away from them.

Dante slowed his pace and glanced uphill. The wild man had followed them, but he now stood at a midway point in the rocks. His eyes combed the trees, but he didn't follow farther. Abruptly, he turned and trudged uphill.

Dropping Lauralee's wrist, Dante swiveled to glare at her. She wasn't facing him. She'd turned toward the hillside and leaned against a tree. "Do you see what your reckless behavior causes? What were you thinking?" He took two steps to reach her because she didn't answer. Then he saw why. Tears coursed down her cheeks, and she began to sob, really sob, as a person would when they'd seen a nightmare. "Hey," he said in a softer tone. "Hey now, hey . . ." And then he enfolded her in his arms.

She realized that Dante was holding her, and she felt his arms around her, but she still trembled with the fear that iced her blood. Most certainly, they were out of danger. Dante wouldn't have stopped running. She asked, just to make sure, "Is he gone?"

"Yes." He breathed hard too. She moved with the rise and fall of his chest, heard his heart pound through his shirt. He pushed her gently and held her at arm's length. "Are you all right?" His jawline was stubbly with a new beard as black as his hair and eyebrows. Though he wasn't his usual salubrious self, Lauralee found him appealing in a manly way.

She nodded and wiped her cheeks with her fingers. "Sorry," she offered and then brightened. "You saved my life . . . again."

"Yes, well, you took about twenty years off mine, thank you

very much." When she continued to grin at him, he drew in his brows and dropped his hands from her shoulders. "Who was that?"

"I think it's Levi." She twisted around to gaze uphill. "I've never actually seen him before, but there's always been talk about him."

"You knew he was here?" She turned to look at him again and he asked, "What are you doing, Lauralee?"

"I came to find you. The most impossible thing has happened. Chief Shank is searching for you." She thought for a moment. "Why are you staying out here? I thought you were going to Denver."

"I can't leave, you know that, not while Emelina is in Victor City."

"But why aren't you in Victor City?"

His eyes flashed in irritation. Without answering, he moved toward the edge of the clearing and toward her horse. "I want you to get out of here."

Confused, she watched him. "But . . . Chief Shank thinks you're a thief. I've come to help you." He held out the reins for her to take but she didn't reach for them. "Come back with me. Talk to my father. He will speak to Shank if you like—"

"Why would he do that?"

"Because Shank listens to him. My father used to be the sheriff. Tell him that you searched for the gypsy the night the jewels were stolen."

"I can't do that."

"I was with you, Dante. I'll help prove that you're innocent."

His eyes widened. "Prove me innocent? You're impossible. Do you know that? You charge out, knowing that a wild man lives here, to tell me something I already know . . . What sort of trusting fool are you?" He dug into his pants pocket and held out his hand. There, in his palm, lay a pair of earrings. From his fingers dangled a pearl necklace.

Lauralee caught her breath and stared at the man she'd misjudged so badly. "You're a *thief?*"

He closed his eyes in impatience and jammed the jewelry into his pocket again.

"What is wrong with you?"

"I like to steal!" he hollered back.

She said in a softer tone, full of wonderment, "That makes no sense. You're a lawyer, a defender of the guiltless. How could you do it?"

With a confused look, he repeated, "Defender of the guiltless . . . ?"

"Did you lie when you told me about the gypsy?"

He shoved the reins at her again without answering.

"Why did you ask my uncle about heredity, Mr. Quinn?"

His dark eyes snapped back to hers. "I don't owe you any explanations."

It was the second time he'd said that, but this time she had a ready answer. "Oh, yes, you do. I believed in you. I defended you."

"I didn't ask you to!"

Anger scorched her insides. "You are the most suspicious, hostile, distrustful *thief* I have ever met."

His nostrils flared. "I will throw you onto this horse if you don't seat yourself on it immediately."

She ignored his threat and leaned against a tall pine. All her anger evaporated and she asked in a quizzical tone, "Why *did* you ask about heredity? Are you concerned that your children will inherit your sticky fingers?"

Dante blinked his eyes as if the shift in the argument's momentum confused him. "I don't have children."

"Or maybe you think you got your sticky fingers from your father . . ." She pushed off the tree and took the horse's reins. "You're criminally ill, I suppose. Uncle Todd will fix you up. We'll need to see him right away."

"No."

"It's your only option." She frowned at him.

He leaned toward her with narrowed black eyes. "I am *not* ill." He was really quite annoyed.

Lauralee felt chastised, and she bit her lip. "Well, you need help, and I will help you."

He wasn't looking at her any longer, but into the distance, at something through the trees and farther down the hill.

Lauralee turned and saw three horsemen galloping toward them.

Without a word, Dante moved into the trees, and in a moment's time, he disappeared.

Dante didn't see Lauralee saddle up. He headed for the boulders that he'd originally used as a lookout. Obviously he couldn't stay in these foothills, not with a reptile-swinging lunatic tramping about. Hunkering between the large rocks, he watched the horsemen. Lauralee rode toward them and reined in.

Now she would prove her deceitfulness, thought Dante, watching with dark fascination. Her back was to him but he could see Lauralee's movements. She lifted her arm and pointed uphill . . .

"He's real. I saw him," Lauralee told the men. She halted her horse in the valley, green and sparkling from the earlier rains. Where the horses had trudged were prints and torn sod.

Chief Shank and Deputies Vaughn and Casillo watched her closely as she caught her breath. Shank asked, "What are you doing out here?" He was a frightful lawman to see, with his brows drawn together. His dark blue eyes were smaller than ever, and they were hard and shrewd.

"I stopped and got off my horse . . . He came out of the trees," she told them, still winded. "He picked up the snake and attacked me . . ."

"Dante Quinn?" the chief asked her, holding tightly to his reins. His horse danced to the left, sensitive to the new rider and mount.

"Levi! He's up there!"

Her statement had the desired affect on both Casillo and Vaughn. Both men shrank backward in their saddles.

Shank, however, didn't act concerned at the news. "There is no Levi."

"Well, what causes those lights up in the hills?" Vaughn wanted to know, sitting forward again. His dark hair curled around his face.

Lauralee shook her head. "Well, maybe his name isn't Levi, but there's a wild man up there. He's blistered and . . . feral." She reworked the tears she'd shed earlier and began to stutter. "I d-dismounted and I heard the s-snake . . ."

"All right, settle down," Shank told her. He studied the hills for a moment while Lauralee wept into her hands. She sneaked a peek at him through her lashes. Suddenly, he stared at her again. "Did you see Dante Quinn?"

Lauralee sniffed. "Quinn, that awful fellow from California? Rick and I saw him yesterday."

"Where?"

"On the trail to our house. He said he was going to Denver.

Why are you looking for Mr. Quinn?" She asked this last bit
because it was something she would normally ask and expect
to get involved in.

Casillo spoke from behind the chief. He was younger than
Vaughn and had short, spiked brown hair. Looking somewhat
relieved, he asked, "Do you want us to head back to town and
wire Denver, sir?"

Shank sat for a long moment in his saddle, staring at the
hills. Then his eyes found Lauralee's. He said to his deputies,
"Go back to town and wire Denver, Sterling, and Forge Rock.
I'll see Lauralee home."

"Lauralee was upset, and I thought to bring her home,
Wade. I found her running away from Fool's Peak. Said she
saw something."

She could feel her father's eyes on her, but he didn't say
anything. He stuck out his hand. "Thank you, Reuben. I appreciate your looking out for her."

"Sure thing. I'm sure you'd look after my boy if you found
him in trouble. And," he added, "you know how young people
are, Wade. They can get themselves into trouble quicker than
a jackrabbit in a carrot race." Shank's small eyes landed on
Lauralee. "Or they *think* they found trouble and in their fervor
start making things up."

Wade Murphy looked between Shank and Lauralee.

Shank sat straighter in the saddle and pulled the reins. "I'll
talk to you again, Lauralee, when you're feeling better."

"Yes," she whispered, nodding her head without looking at
the chief. "Thank you again for seeing me home."

They moved toward the house and her father casually
asked, "What were you doing at Fool's Peak?"

Shank had already pushed his horse toward the road when

Lauralee glanced at her father. She never lied to him—didn't think she could, for that matter—so she said, "I thought I saw Dante Quinn ride off that way yesterday."

Wade Murphy stopped walking before Lauralee did. When she noticed it, she turned to face him in the yard between the house and the corral. He asked, "The man the chief is looking for?"

"That's who I was looking for, but I found Levi instead." Lauralee nearly choked on the untruth.

"Levi?" He used the same tone Reuben Shank had used when he'd said the name.

"I don't know if he was the Levi everybody talks about in town, but the fellow was huge and blistered." She shifted her weight, waiting for her father's response.

"Is that right?"

This he said with the tiniest bit of danger in it.

Lauralee gaped at him. "He picked up a snake and shook it at me."

"How'd you get away from him?"

"Ran . . . fast . . . Will you excuse me?"

An awkward silence followed, during which her father held her eyes for a long moment, as if searching for something there. Then he nodded and said, "Sure."

Chapter Eight

I heard you were out by Fool's Peak yesterday, Miss Murphy."

They sat in her father's study, with its dark paneling and bookshelf along the wall. The sun came from the west windows, for it was later in the day, just before nightfall. Lauralee was in the big leather seat near the window. She'd been there before her father walked in and Ewing had arrived. She stayed only because the newspaperman told her not to go, that he wouldn't be long and had only a few questions for her father. She regarded the man and set aside her book.

He asked, "What were you doing out there?"

"I often ride in different directions."

"Deputy Vaughn said you thought you saw a ghost."

That was the reason for the visit, Lauralee determined, watching Ewing carefully. He'd come under the guise of interviewing her father. "I never claimed to see a ghost."

Ewing turned his watery eyes on Wade Murphy. "I'm surprised you let her roam the countryside unattended. Who knows what could happen to her?"

"Lauralee's a fine horsewoman," her father said, taking a

seat behind his wide desk and holding out a hand for Ewing to take a seat. "She manages fine on her own. I trust her completely."

Her chest tightened at his words as a fresh wave of remorse seized her. She didn't look at her father, but she knew he watched her.

Dressed in a gray suit coat and pants, Felton looked more sharklike than ever. He'd smoothed his blond hair back with oil, and Lauralee could see streaks of the stuff around his ear. He asked, "It doesn't bother you that she met a crazy man?"

Her father smiled patiently. "I thought you said 'ghost.' "

"There are other stories circulating around town."

Wade Murphy held the man's eyes for a small moment. "What happened at Fool's Peak is a family matter."

"You'd best forget that excuse if you're to be governor," Ewing responded. "Your business is everyone's business." He glanced at Lauralee again. "Didn't I see you eating dinner with Dante Quinn the other evening?"

"What evening was that?" she asked, stomach tingling. She sat straighter in the chair and chanced a glance at her father. He waited quietly, seeming to take in the atmosphere of the room, noting Felton's demeanor, and then his eyes fell to Lauralee's twisting fingers. She stopped immediately and gripped the arms of the chair.

"Oh, sometime last week."

"I didn't eat dinner with Dante Quinn."

Felton insisted, "But you were with him at Marigold's . . ."

"With Chief Shank and Dante Quinn, yes." It wasn't exactly a lie. Shank did show up. Eventually. "Are you keeping tabs on me, Mr. Ewing?" She glanced at her father. He leaned backward in his chair with his fingers crossed in front of him. Lauralee glowered at Felton Ewing again.

He hadn't lost his slick grin. "Oh, I'm as nosy as can be; that's me. It's my nature, I suppose, and probably why I chose the profession I did."

"I suppose," Lauralee agreed, gaining her feet, and closing her book. "If you'll excuse me."

"Oh, but—" he began, rising too.

Wade Murphy cut him off. "I thought you came to speak to me, Felton. Have a seat."

Add that to the reasons she loved her father so much.

Cool air came off the mountains. It tempered the warm air in the valley, where Long Winter Ranch spread out between Wolf Whistle Creek and the Martin River. Between them was a thousand acres of woodlands filled with mist. Rivers turned into falls. Ponderosa pines stood tall along the hills. Lauralee walked toward White Basker Knoll intending to watch the stars come out. Smooth blackness stretched across the horizon; golden beams touched the western edge of the mountains like a woman's slender fingers reaching toward the heavens.

Evergreens grew thicker as she neared the knoll, and it was from them that a man stepped out in front of Lauralee. She drew back, ready to scream, but somehow she sensed it was Dante Quinn—possibly because he'd sneaked up on her previously. He whispered, "I have to speak to you."

"Fine," she said, trying to catch her breath. "Cat burglar suits you, by the way. What with how you *pounce* on a person . . ." She took a gulp of air to slow her heartbeat. It was going that fast.

"Well, I couldn't very well walk up to the front door and knock, now could I? I've been waiting out here all day for you as it is." He pushed something at her.

"What's this?"

"A razor. I stole it from one of the men in the bunkhouse."

"It's a good start, returning things." She slipped the pouch into her skirt pocket. "Did you bathe as well?" She asked because she could smell the residue of soap on him and the fresh scent of his hair.

"I did, in the creek."

Though she could make out only the square-shouldered shadow of him, Lauralee enjoyed the sense of him. Dante's black eyes were lost to her in the darkness, but they reached for her, she knew, perhaps only from memory, and she felt his warmth. "You should leave. Shank is still looking for you. He could show up any time." She stepped closer to Dante, to speak softly. "I don't think he believed me when I told him I hadn't seen you. And don't go to Denver. He's wired the police there."

It surprised her when Dante's hand reached for hers and his fingers held on firmly. "Why did you lure them away?" There was no longer urgency in his tone, but something else: appreciation, trustfulness.

"Is that what you came here to ask?"

"Why?" His finger squeezed hers, and he took another step toward her.

He needed to leave, but suddenly she didn't want him to go. "Because I . . . I don't believe you're— I mean I understand you're a thief, but I cannot believe you're all bad. You've saved my life twice."

"You think you owe me?"

She reached for his arm and placed her free hand on the sleeve of his shirt. "I think you need help."

"You're right. I do need help. I need you to find Emelina for me."

She hesitated, disturbed by his reply. "You'll risk Shank finding you, imprisonment, just to find Emelina Istok?"

"I don't have a choice."

Lauralee said what she had thought for some time now. "She's your mama, isn't she? You're not chasing her because she caused someone's death."

"She killed my father." Dante dropped her hand and took a step away from her.

"You said he drank."

"Because she left. When I was six years old, she wrote a note to my father—the poor trusting wretch that he was. She said she missed her gypsy life." His tone sounded angrier as he spoke. And hurt. "She took off, and my father grabbed a bottle for comfort. I didn't have that luxury."

"How old were you when he died?"

"Ten."

Oh, thought Lauralee as she realized he'd been left on his own at such a young age. *He would be the same age as her cousin Daniel when Mary had died. What if Todd left Daniel alone?* Lauralee reached and found Dante's arm again. "Who raised you?"

"It doesn't matter."

"It does matter, Dante. It's the reason you don't trust anybody."

His laugh sounded low, harsh. "Oh, I'm much more specific a person than that, Lauralee."

"You don't trust women." He didn't deny it, only stood still there in front of her. She could feel the tense muscles of his forearm through the material of his shirtsleeve. "Yet you're willing to trust me?"

"Never with my heart, dear girl. Never that."

It disappointed her that he admitted it. With all her being she wished she could change his mind. Letting loose of his sleeve, she stepped away from him. "So . . . you're a gypsy?"

"Half Roma," he insisted bitterly. "I've tried all my life to conceal it."

"Why?"

"You're very naive, aren't you? Are you so protected here that you don't know what gypsies are or what people think of them? No one wants a gypsy for a lawyer."

She nodded. "So you steal in order to get people to trust you?"

"The thieving is a new development," he answered impatiently.

"You didn't always steal? Why did you start?"

She saw the shadow of his face turn toward the house as if he was gathering his thoughts. Maybe he didn't think she would believe him. "She cursed me."

"Who?"

"Emelina."

"Your own mama cursed you?"

"Yes . . . yes, she chanted a bunch of nonsense at me, and now I steal things."

"That's possible?"

"Apparently," he said with a hint of sarcasm.

"You're saying you can't help yourself?"

"I'm saying that I don't know when I do it. I wake in the morning and the jewelry is there."

"You steal in your sleep?"

"Apparently." He spun away from her and faced the path that led to the house and barns.

Lauralee moved to his side. "So, you're trying to find Emelina so that she'll lift the curse?"

"Yes . . . No. I don't believe in curses."

"Oh, sure, me neither." Small light from the moon and stars reflected off his fine features. She wanted to trace her finger along his scowling brows. "Then why are you searching for her?"

"You wouldn't understand." He turned his face toward hers again. "You have your parents, your life. You're happy and whole. I want that too."

"How can Emelina give that to you?"

He didn't answer at first, but then in a rush, he said, "I want to know why, okay? I want to know why she left me. What did I do?"

"You were six; what could you have possibly—"

"I must've done something. Why would she prefer the gypsy life to taking care of her son, whom she swore she loved so very much?"

Lauralee bit her lip. It needed to be said, and she said it: "Maybe you should forget about her, Dante. Anyone who can call a tornado out of the sky is no one to chase after . . . Talk to my uncle about your sleepwalking."

"No." He found her hand again. "I don't expect you to understand. Just find her for me. She's still in town. She came here for a reason."

When he said it, Lauralee remembered something. "Do you know anyone named Esme Beckett?"

"Esme? No."

"I saw her the other day and she acted so strange when I mentioned that a gypsy got off the train." Lauralee stepped closer to him, excited that she might know a clue to the gypsy's whereabouts. "I think Emelina asks her for money now and then. I don't know what their connection is—"

"She's hiding her?"

"I doubt it. Esme acted scared of Emelina."

"Where does she live?"

"Wolf Whistle Creek, but I don't think she's there. When Esme met her son in town, they went straight to the church."

"The church," he said enthusiastically. "You think the church is hiding Emelina?"

Lauralee shook her head. "I doubt Pastor Carmichael is hiding her, but maybe he's taken pity on her. She's old. She can't live on the street."

"Well, she's not at the hotel or anywhere else. I searched every corner of town."

"But did you look inside the church?"

He sighed. "I went inside, but there was no one there. I didn't search the place, as it seemed irreverent somehow."

Happy with her inductive skills, Lauralee smiled. "I'll bet that's where she is. All we have to do is get you inside the church."

"I can't chance that, Lauralee, not with Shank looking for me." His hands found her upper arms and he pulled her closer. "Bring her here, Lauralee."

"Bring her here . . . how?"

"I don't know. Befriend her. Offer her a place to stay. When she's here, I can talk to her, reasonably and calmly."

"But how do I befriend her?"

"I've watched you. People like you; they trust you." His face moved closer to hers and she felt his breath on her lips. "You're my only hope. Will you do it?"

Put like that, coupled with the way he'd pulled her close, his request caused Lauralee's heart to beat a new rhythm. His lips came ever closer. "Will you?" he asked again.

She nodded, and his lips touched hers only briefly before a twig snapped on their left. Dante pulled away and stared into the trees. Another noise sounded, and Dante dropped his hands.

"I've got to go inside," Lauralee told him. "Where will I find you?"

The sun shone through a roof of pine leaves swaying in a light wind above their heads. Piper stood on the bank while Lauralee sat in a bower made by a tree. Naberling Creek flowed low and broad before them. On the other side of the bank and up a winding path stood the back of Victor City Church.

"You're in love with him?" Piper meant Dante Quinn. It was whom they discussed while watching for some sign of the gypsy in back of the church.

"In love? Goodness. Just because he *barely* kissed me doesn't mean I love him."

"I didn't mean because he kissed you, barely or otherwise. Did you *want* him to kiss you?"

Lauralee pulled at a blade of grass and folded it at its vein. "Yes."

"Any woman in her right mind would want him to; he has the face of a theater star."

Lauralee gaped at her. "He's more than handsome. He's brave. He's saved my life—"

"Twice."

She frowned at Piper. "But that's not even the point. I don't care that he's handsome and brave. Dante is . . . hurting inside."

"He's going to hurt a lot more when the chief catches him. He'll go to jail, Lauralee. He's a thief."

"I told you why he steals."

Piper faced her fully. "But he's a fugitive. Think of your future children . . . little felons running around . . ."

"I'm not going to marry him. I just want to help him."

Piper turned to peer at the church again. "Why can't we go over and ask Pastor Carmichael if the gypsy's there?"

"He won't tell us, if she's requested sanctuary."

"Why would she do that?"

Lauralee got to her feet and brushed the back of her long skirt. "Because she knew Dante was searching for her." She stood beside Piper and watched the back of the building across the river. "Maybe if you distract the pastor while I sneak in the back way, I can find her."

"Do you hear yourself? Are you unhampered by the moral dilemma of *sneaking* into a church?"

Lauralee blinked at her.

"That's what happens when your beau is a felon."

"He's not my beau . . ."

Piper wasn't listening to her. She tilted her head and watched the trees. All at once, she grabbed Lauralee's sleeve.

"What's the matter?"

"I thought I saw something."

She peered at the wild grass and laurel across the path. A gray cloud drifted across the sun, and a curious breeze sighed through the pines. Shadows darkened in the narrow gaps between the trees.

Something slipped passed on their left.

Piper's hand tightened on her arm.

And then Emelina Istok stood there, just to the right of them and only a couple of feet away. She wore the same purple skirt and dingy white blouse as she did the first time Lauralee had seen her, but she'd draped a red shawl around her shoulders and wore a black scarf around her head. A long strand of beads fell from her neck. The blood-drop stone still hung around her neck.

Dante's mother. He had her eyes, though Emelina's were lighter in color. They both had thick dark brows. Lauralee supposed mother and son resembled each other, but she couldn't help but think Emelina resembled someone else too. It was the way the old gypsy stood there that reminded Lauralee of . . . Esme Beckett.

She said, "My *natsia* has come, and I wish to join them."

"What's a not-see-ya?" Piper asked, still gripping Lauralee hard.

"My people."

Lauralee asked her, "Where are they?"

The gypsy took a step forward. "They are near the wolf's creek."

"Do you think she means Wolf Whistle?" Piper whispered.

That made sense, because Esme Beckett lived there. Lauralee asked, "Do you want to see someone there?"

"My clan, yes. They have come." She took another step forward. Lauralee realized the woman meant that the caravan had come, the gypsy caravan that helped with the harvest. But how did Emelina know they'd come? Did Esme and Oliver tell her? Emelina ventured, "I have no way to travel unless you take me there."

"Why don't you come home with me instead?" Lauralee asked, pulling away from Piper's grip. "My family will shelter you and feed you."

The old woman shook her head. "I want to be with *my* family. Take me to them and I will tell your fortune. We will consult the sphere and read the cards."

Lauralee didn't know how to convince Emelina differently. If she took her to Wolf Whistle Creek, then she would at least know where to tell Dante to find her. "All right. We'll take you there."

"We will?" Piper asked.

"Sure," Lauralee said, returning Piper's wide stare. "You'd like to see a gypsy camp, wouldn't you?"

"Who wouldn't?"

Lauralee glanced at Emelina Istok and pointed through the trees. "I have a buggy in front of my uncle's home. We'll take you to your people."

The day turned windy, and shadows of clouds sailed over the floor of the valley. The gypsy sat between Lauralee and Piper. Lauralee held the reins to the day buggy and urged the horses toward Wolf Whistle Creek. In the distance she saw the lower lands dotted with small clumps of trees. And there ran the wild mustangs. The blackest of them was in the lead. How Lauralee wished her father were with her now. He'd chased the black stallion for years and never caught him.

Piper watched with Lauralee for a moment and then turned to ask the old woman, "You travel with your family?"

"I travel with different families. All gypsies are my family."

"That's a lot of people to cook dinner for . . ."

"We Roma wander on the earth," Emelina continued. "But it was not always so. We come from another land that was long ago destroyed."

"Romania?" Piper asked, looking at Lauralee. "Isn't Romania still in one piece?"

"Do not confuse us with Romanian people. I speak of Zott on the Tigris River." Lauralee noticed that the gypsy didn't speak to Piper but stared off into the distance, toward the creek. "One day a man came to our camp and we invited him in. This was our mistake and was to be our curse. He wanted us to serve him, but we refused. We love life. In a rage he cursed us, saying that we would forever wander. We would never settle in any land, and we would forever be banished. The man disappeared, and we laughed at him and his foretelling."

"And then what happened?" Piper asked, on the edge of her seat.

"Our land was destroyed by fire."

"Fire?"

"Yes, a great fire that destroyed all of the land. Those who survived ran away onto a mountain. Gathering, we drew a circle, and all there drew knives and shed blood on the earth. When the last drop soaked into the ground a strange feeling came over us. The land embraced us. A voice told us that we would be cursed to wander, yes, but we now had the ability to curse those who would cause our death. We have wandered ever since." With the last of the story, Emelina grew quiet, and she watched the hills in the distance.

"Well . . . *wow*," Piper said, and she threw Lauralee a look over the gypsy's head that suggested *what a bunch of twaddle.*

They rolled along on level ground, and the lane, after much winding, lay straight ahead through the grassland dotted with tall trees. A gray ribbon of creek came into view. To the north was the Wolf Whistle Creek community. To the south, Lauralee saw a group of wagons in the shade of the pawpaw trees. People milled about. Children played. She heard a faint note of viola music on the breeze.

A man sat on the steps at the back of one of the wagons. His feet dangled while he whittled on a piece of wood. When he saw the buggy, he set the wood aside, but not the knife. He called out loudly and hopped from the steps. Arms flailing, he called his people around him. The man appeared to be in his fifties, and a thick mustache grew beneath his wide nose.

Children quieted. One by one they moved to the far end of the camp and away from the visitors. The music ceased.

Lauralee pulled on the reins, and the horse dug its hooves into the damp ground. It whinnied when another man stepped forward and took hold of the halter straps. Twenty or so men and women stood behind the man who'd called them forward. The women dressed in skirts, different colors all of them, with blouses that did not necessarily match the color of their skirts. Some wore scarves over their long, dark hair. The men wore long-sleeved shirts, pants, and colored vests. All of them, men and women, wore cautiousness about them and exchanged dark looks among them. This seemed odd to Lauralee. Any time in the past when she had visited the camp, the people welcomed strangers warmly.

But it seemed the gypsies' interest was not in Lauralee or Piper, but in Emelina Istok. And they did not appear happy to see her. The man who'd seen them first stepped forward and spoke directly to Emelina in the Roma language so that Lauralee did not understand him. His tone sounded strict.

As for Emelina, she spoke confidently to the man. No, more than confidently, she spoke arrogantly to him, and he frowned deeply at her.

Then from the crowd stepped a young woman. Her black hair fell splendidly down her back. She appeared young, in her twenties perhaps, and she was a beguiling enchantress. Beautiful. She locked eyes with Emelina while she spoke to the man. Lauralee didn't understand anything the young woman said except *Istok*.

The man didn't look any happier, but he held out his hand as if to welcome Emelina. To Lauralee, he said, "You are welcome to refresh your horse."

Piper moved first and stood aside while the old gypsy climbed from the buggy. The beautiful girl stepped forward and held out her arm for Emelina to take. Lauralee stepped out of the buggy too and stood next to Piper. To the man, she quietly said, "Thank you."

He didn't seem to acknowledge that she had spoke, and he turned his back to climb the steps to the wagon again. The men and women backed away too, to return to whatever they were doing before they were called together. Emelina, however, spoke to the young woman who'd helped her from the buggy. Suddenly, she turned around to watch Lauralee and Piper. "I am with my family now. But I promised to tell your future, *va?*"

"No need," Lauralee told her. "You read my palm the other night, remember?"

"This is Roza. She is *Kalderasha* in her blood, as I am." She turned and spoke to Roza again, and the young woman smiled—but not warmly.

"Come," Roza said. "Marko will take your horse." She nodded to a young man who still held the reins to the day buggy. He moved swiftly to unhitch the animal.

Lauralee and Piper followed Roza toward one of the wagons. It was barrel-topped and painted blue. Stairs led to a small round door next to a window with flowers streaming from its box.

"Sit," Roza told them, pointing to a small table that jutted from the wall of the wagon. "Phuro will speak to Casamir now."

"Who is Phuro?" Lauralee asked.

"The old woman who brought you here."

"I thought her name was Emelina Istok."

Roza twirled to face Lauralee. "Phuro to you is 'aged,' *va?*"

"And who is Casamir?" Lauralee asked, gazing out the curtained door window.

"Our father here. He who gathers us with one word is Casamir."

Lauralee understood that the man she'd first seen was

Casamir. She gazed about the wagon. It was larger inside than she'd expected. Wood panels made up the walls of it, and a small bed was built into the back. Roza took her seat at the table and motioned to them.

While Piper sat in front of her, Lauralee continued to watch outside the window. Emelina Istok stood near the first wagon with the man Casamir. He'd picked up his wood piece and whittled again, but now he held the knife differently. Instead of shaving at the wood, he chopped at it.

"We will read the cards," Roza told Piper. "We will see your future in romantics, *va?*"

"Oh, yes," cooed Piper, leaning forward eagerly.

"Seven of spades: Someone will offer you advice. Do not take it."

Piper turned to Lauralee with wide green eyes. "Help me remember that."

Roza dealt another card. "Ten of diamonds: Happiness will soon come. A problem will have a joyful ending. That is *bak,* eh: lucky?"

Lauralee cast a look out the window again. Casamir looked no happier—less so, as a matter of fact. Emelina spoke to him, leaning toward him, and he nodded his head. Roza snapped another card on the table in front of Piper. "Seven of diamonds: Think about something that you've never thought to do." She laid one more card out and smiled coyly. "Nine of hearts," she said softly. "It is a wish card."

"A wish?" Piper asked in excitement.

"Yes, and the card before it is a diamond. That means your wish will come true. It will be fulfilled."

Piper turned to Lauralee. "Did you hear that? I get a wish."

Lauralee nodded and gazed out the window again.

Roza rose to her feet to stand next to Lauralee. She was the same height as Lauralee but more slender, and certainly more bewitching, with her lush curls and sable eyes. Her cherry-red blouse dipped low onto her bosom. Gold chains lay there and on both her wrists. She wore large hoop earrings. She asked Lauralee, "What are you watching, eh?"

Lauralee nodded toward the old gypsy woman. "I just want to make sure that she's all right. I can take her to my home."

"She is family here."

"Who don't seem happy to see her," Lauralee pointed out.

Roza cast a look out the window as well. "That is because they fear her. She is powerful with her magic and knows the old ways."

"Will she stay here?"

"Yes."

Lauralee thought a moment. "If someone wants to live here, any of your family, any Roma, do you always accept them?"

A thick line of kohl ran along the bottom of her eyes. "Yes. We make sure they are Roma, but we accept them."

"How do you make sure?"

"We will send someone to check with other clans in the area." She moved in front of the door, swinging her skirt as she positioned herself there. "But I always know Roma when I see them. I have a sense for this. It is a skill, *va?*" She put her hand on the doorknob.

"Do you have any love potions?" Piper broke in cheerfully, standing now.

Lauralee frowned at her friend and then asked Roza, "What if a person cannot prove they're Roma?"

"Do you want to be gypsy?" she asked in a sly tone, tilting her head. Her black curls tumbled off her shoulder.

"Me? No," Lauralee told her and then added quickly, "I mean no offense." She thought to go at this in a new direction.

"What if someone is wanted by the law? Do you protect that person?"

Roza opened the door and held it for them. "We have our own laws. Our own ways. See, Marko has brought your horse to your buggy. It is time for you to go, *va?*"

"Wait," Piper insisted. "What about the love potion?"

She flipped the reins, and the horse turned left to trot in a wide circle. Lauralee directed it toward the lane that led back to the winding road toward Victor City. They weren't on the trail too long before Piper asked, "Why did you want to take the gypsy home with you so badly?"

"Why did you want a love potion?" Lauralee asked, to quickly change the conversation.

Piper laughed. "For fun. I wanted to try it out and see if it works." She held the small pouch in her lap and glanced at it. "Now if I can remember the correct words . . ."

"What's in the pouch?"

Piper shrugged. "Leaves, I think. But they're special leaves. They must have potion on them."

"Open it up." When Piper separated the strings, Lauralee glanced inside. "They're laurel leaves. What did she tell you to do?"

"Sit before a dying fire and gaze into it. Clear my mind of all but thoughts of my dearest love. Put the leaves in a small basket and hold it between my knees."

"Why a small basket?"

Piper frowned at her. "I don't know. It's part of the magic, I suppose. I'm to keep gazing into the fire, dip my left hand into the basket . . ."

"What happens if you dip your right hand into the basket?"

"I don't know. Now concentrate and help me remember all

of this. I'm to take a handful of leaves and toss them into the fire. As they burst into flame, I have to chant out loud, 'Laurel leaves that burn in the fire, draw unto me my heart's desire.' "

"That's just silly."

Piper shrugged happily.

"And whom do you propose to put a love spell on anyway?"

"Er . . . I don't know. I'm not picky."

Lauralee knew exactly whom Piper had in mind, but she said, "So you'll settle for Felton Ewing, is that it? Are you going to think about his downy blond hair while dipping your left hand into the basket?"

"Good heavens," Piper said, aghast. "His bird-calling piccolo would put me over a cliff." She bit her lip and considered the pouch in her lap. "I was thinking of someone a bit handsomer than Ewing."

"Ugly men need love too," Lauralee told her.

"Yes, but I'm not going to waste my love potion on the ugly."

"All right, what about Rowdy Taylor?" After Piper shrugged, Lauralee suggested, "Efren Vaughn?"

Piper shrugged again. "I'll let the love potion decide for me. How about that?"

"Of course. Who better to chose our husbands for us than a stack of laurel leaves?"

"Then you'll do it with me?" she asked in excitement. "It looks as though I have plenty of leaves."

"Er . . . no. I really need to get home quickly," she told her, thinking to find Dante before the sun went down.

"All right. How about I come to your house and after dinner we can try it out for ourselves?"

Piper was always a welcome addition at her home, and Lauralee didn't know how she could possibly turn her down. It would be easy to sneak away from her for a few moments to find

Dante by the river and tell him where Emelina was staying. And if she couldn't get home in time this evening, she would go in the morning to find Dante. Piper would probably want to spend some time with Rick anyway, gathering enough thoughts to use for her love potion. "That's fine by me that you stay the night."

Sunlight filtering through the curtains woke Lauralee early, and she dressed in a beige-colored riding skirt and white button-down blouse. She left her hair down because there wasn't time to pile it on top of her head. Moving downstairs, she walked outside and went quickly to the barn.

She wanted an early start and had slept later than she meant to. When she'd finally escaped Piper last evening, the sky had already turned dark. Lauralee didn't like riding in the forest at night by herself, so she walked to the knoll in hopes that Dante would find her again.

He didn't.

Day had come pale from the east. Heather covered the slopes in the near distance. Farther, hills faded into the far-off blue. Only halfway to the barn, Lauralee stopped walking when she saw a horseman riding swiftly toward the house. When the man was close enough, she saw that it was Rowdy Taylor, one of the ranch hands, and he yanked the reins hard when he drew near the paddock fence where Rick stood with two ranch hands.

Rowdy handed Rick the weekly paper—he actually handed him two—and spoke enthusiastically. Her brother opened the paper, and all four men leaned in to see it, and then in a most extraordinary manner, they all turned toward Lauralee.

Rick stomped forward, his face rigid.

"What in the world is the matter with you?" Lauralee asked, stepping to the side before he plowed her over. He didn't answer, only shoved one of the newspapers into her hands and then marched toward the house.

She stared after him. Lifting the paper, she gazed at the front page. Her heart stopped as she read the words: WADE MURPHY UNFIT FOR GOVERNORSHIP. Beneath, it read: *Lauralee Murphy Seen in the Arms of Fugitive Dante Quinn.*

Felton Ewing, Lauralee thought. He'd seen her on the knoll with Dante Quinn? Had he heard their whole conversation or only parts of it? It didn't matter. Lauralee Murphy was in terrible, terrible trouble.

Chapter Nine

Lauralee knew now what it felt like to face Sheriff Wade Murphy rather than Papa. As sheriff his sternness nearly left her breathless. She wilted under his flat stare.

Taking a moment to feel sorry for herself, she wondered what he must think of her. Certainly he was disappointed. Definitely he was angry. He said, "You saw Dante Quinn. You met him."

"I didn't set out to meet him. He was on the knoll."

"Dante Quinn was on our property and you said nothing." He stood in the middle of the study facing Lauralee, who sat at his wide desk. It was where she'd landed when she'd flown into the room searching for him. He'd been waiting for her with a second copy of the *Gazette* in his hands.

"He asked me to help him," she said in a small voice.

"Why you?"

"Because I saw the gypsy. Dante is searching for her."

Wade Murphy held up his hand to halt her explanation. "Forget the gypsy. I want you to tell me about your relationship with Quinn."

127

"I don't have a *relationship* . . . ," she started to explain, her heart nearly failing inside her chest.

He tossed the newspaper on the desk. "Is this a lie?"

"Of course it is. You're certainly fit to be governor."

"Lauralee!"

She held her breath.

It seemed he fought the urge to shout. "Did the two of you embrace?"

"Not *exactly*."

His eyes narrowed. "Not exactly? Why don't you tell me *exactly* what is going on then."

"He asked me to find the gypsy and bring her here so that he could confront her." Her words came out in a rush. "She's his mother, and she's cursed him."

He placed his hands on the desk and leaned toward her. "So he has family problems. That doesn't mean he's not a thief, Lauralee."

"Oh," she said brightly. "I *know* he's a thief."

For a long moment he stared at her. "Where is he?"

"I . . . I don't know exactly," she told him evasively. "The last I saw him he was on Fool's Peak."

It might've been a mistake to mention that.

"You lied to Shank."

She felt her stomach fluttering around inside her. "No, no, I didn't. Levi really is there. I saw him."

Her father's face went rigid. "You lied to me."

"I didn't." She got to her feet, flushing hotly. "I just didn't tell you that I saw him."

A knock sounded and Rick stuck his head around the door. He didn't look at Lauralee but spoke to their father. "Judge Mitchell's here."

Wade Murphy took a deep breath while watching Lauralee, and then he turned. "Show him in." Glancing at her again, he said, "Why don't you go on. We'll talk later."

Lauralee took the back way out of his office to the hallway, where a narrow flight of steps led to the top floor. She'd just snapped the door shut when she heard Mitchell's thunderous voice. "Is this true, Murphy?"

Her father gave a soft reply, and she leaned against the door. Stinging tears bubbled in her eyes, and the sick feeling she'd had in her father's office came back vengefully.

"Have you spoken to the fool girl?" the judge asked, wanting to know, not bothering to be tactful about it.

She could imagine her father's crestfallen features. "He's using her. The man is using her . . ."

"Lauralee has always been a bit raw about the edges," the judge put in. "What will you do, Wade?"

Lauralee leaned harder against the door to hear the answer. "Drop out of the race."

She turned the knob and pushed into the room. "No, Papa . . . you can't drop out of the race."

Mitchell and her father frowned at her as she stood between them in front of the desk.

"You can't," she pleaded, but Wade Murphy said nothing. He rounded the desk and took a seat in the chair. "It's not fair," Lauralee told him softly.

"Well, maybe that's something you should have thought about before you began your romance with Quinn," the judge told her bluntly. Her father cleared his throat, and Mitchell glanced his way. His frothy brows rose nearly to his gray hairline. "It's true, by God . . . though not my place to say. Excuse my outburst, Wade."

"Papa! You're not serious."

"Of course I am. Denver will hear the story soon enough, and the campaign will fail."

Mitchell turned to sit in one of the leather chairs beside the window. "I'm sure Ewing has wired the story to Denver by now."

The tears fell freely now. "It's not fair. You didn't do anything wrong." And before she made an utter idiot of herself, she rushed out of the room and climbed the stairs to her bedroom.

Piper, who had come to visit, was still asleep. She lay on the far side of the bed near the window with pillows scattered about her. A colorful quilt twisted around her slender frame, causing her to look like a patchwork snowman with red hair sticking out the top of it.

Lauralee didn't wake her. Instead she stood in the middle of the room with her chest so tight she could barely breathe. Thoughts whirled through her mind. A sob escaped her, and she bit hard on her lip. Everyone had been right about her all along. She was horribly gullible, far too trusting, and now look at the mess she'd created. Not once had she considered that someone else could get hurt because she tried to help Dante Quinn.

Moving toward the window seat, Lauralee sat and gazed into the yard and out toward the dirt road. She supposed she had to tell Chief Shank that Dante camped somewhere near the river and then confess to him that she'd seen him at Fool's Peak. Perhaps she could make an apology to the people of Victor City . . .

There was still dampness on the window, and Lauralee rubbed a streak with her finger on the pane. Maybe she should ride to Denver and give an interview to the newspapers there.

She didn't trust Ewing to get the story accurate after she gave an apology.

Lauralee pushed off the seat to pace the floor. Should she turn in Dante Quinn herself, make a citizen's arrest, and over-turn Ewing's report in the eyes of the voters? In her heart, she knew she couldn't do that; she couldn't use Dante Quinn the way her father believed Dante had used her.

But he hadn't used her.

Yes, Dante had asked her to sit with him at dinner to find out if any Roma people lived in the immediate area, and yes, the night before last he'd asked her to bring Emelina to Long Winter Ranch, but in Lauralee's mind, Quinn using her would've in-volved money or food in exchange for information. He'd never asked for any of those things. He'd stubbornly tried to do everything on his own.

Dante must turn himself in. It was the only answer. Then Lauralee would make a public apology and beg voters not to blame Wade Murphy for her indiscretions. Movement through the window caught her attention. Horsemen approached on the north road.

Chief Shank.

"Piper," Lauralee said sharply to wake her friend. "Piper, get up now. We've got to go."

The girl twisted in the blanket and then bolted straight up when Lauralee said her name once more. Her reddish curls framed her face, and she brushed at them with one hand. "What's the matter?"

"We've got to sneak out the back way so that Shank doesn't see us." She pulled the covers off the bed and then reached for Piper's small bag. "We've got to find Dante Quinn."

"Where is he?"

"By the river, somewhere, or back at Fool's Peak." She pulled out a pair of riding breeches and a green shirt to throw at her friend. "Get dressed quickly. The chief will be here in a moment's time."

Piper reached for her clothes but not quickly. "You want to go to Fool's Peak?"

"Quiet," she warned. "We have to find Dante and tell him to turn himself in."

"What about Levi?" She stood and pulled the breeches on beneath her long nightgown.

Lauralee gazed around the room and then walked toward the bureau. "I'll take my rifle."

"Are you sure you want to do this?" She'd stopped buttoning the blouse and stared at Lauralee.

"All right. Don't come. Go back to bed." She took the rifle from its place on the wall. "Just don't tell anyone where I'm going." She moved toward the door.

"Wait," Piper insisted. "I'm coming with you."

They rode across the wide hollow. On the far side was a faint path leading to the floor of the forest. Looking ahead, Lauralee could see only tree trunks of countless sizes and shapes with moss, and slippery, bushy saplings.

When they'd rode farther, they picked their way among the trees, and their horses plodded along, carefully avoiding the exposed roots. There was no undergrowth. The ground was rising steadily, and as they went forward it seemed that the trees became taller, darker, and thicker. There was no sound, except an occasional drip of moisture falling through the leaves.

"I can see why you didn't want to come this way by yourself," Piper told her, keeping her mount close to Lauralee's. "It's as if the woods have eyes."

Her friend's words sent a thrill down her spine, for that was exactly what she'd been thinking herself. Then, in the distance, she heard the sound of water. They'd found the river. Surely Dante would remain by the falls. He could bathe there and drink there too.

The light grew clearer as they went forward. Suddenly they came out of the trees and found themselves in a wide circular space. There was Dante by the river, in the green shade of the woods. Mist still hung on the water, and his black hair looked wet with it. When he saw her, his eyes brightened, and he stood to greet them.

Lauralee got off her horse. He met her there and took both her arms. "Did you find Emelina?"

"Yes."

"Is she at your home? Let's go."

He meant to put his foot in the stirrup, but Lauralee stopped him. "Dante, wait. She's not at the ranch."

"Where is she?" He studied Piper, who'd remained on her horse.

Lauralee nodded at her friend. "This is Piper McKinney. You can trust her."

She didn't know whether he believed her or not, because he dismissed Piper quickly and asked, "Where is Emelina?"

She recognized the look he gave her. It was distrust. She'd seen it in his eyes all along, and now her father had worn the same expression. She told Dante, "I'm not going to take you to her . . ."

"Why?" His dark eyes flashed in anger. "What did she say to you?"

"She didn't say anything . . . I want you to turn yourself in."

He guffawed. Disbelief caused his brows to slant together. "Turn myself—"

"It's my father. He's in trouble. He's going to drop out of the governor's race because the editor of the *Victor Gazette* saw you and me together the other night. He wrote a horrible article about how my father isn't fit to be governor because his daughter runs with a felon. Shank's at my house right now ready to question me."

Dante stared hard, but then he shook his head. He said quietly, "I'm sorry for your trouble, Lauralee. Really, I am. But I can't turn myself in. Shank will laugh at me if I tell him that I have a gypsy curse on me, and that's why I steal. He'd throw me in jail without hearing me out."

Piper interrupted, "Wait, you've got a curse on you?" She stared at Lauralee. "You didn't tell me about that."

It was while Dante studied Piper that Lauralee pulled the rifle from the scabbard. When he glanced at her again, surprise flared across his face. Lauralee said, "I'm sorry, too, Dante. But I can't let my father take the blame for this. He's a good man, and he doesn't deserve to be mocked and forced to drop out of the race."

"Put it down," he told her coldly, watching her, and surely seeing that she trembled.

She lifted the weapon higher. "Please believe me when I tell you that I know how to use this. I don't want to hurt you."

"You won't shoot me."

She jacked a shell into the chamber. "Where's your horse?"

He seemed unflustered by her actions. He took measured steps toward the river but kept his eyes on her. "I don't have a horse."

"Get on mine."

He hesitated as if he had no intention of doing what she asked. But he moved forward, to put his foot in the stirrup, and then he dropped and kicked Lauralee's feet out from under her. In a flurry of movement, Dante ripped the rifle from her hand and pointed it at her.

Piper screamed.

"Shut up!" he told her and grabbed Lauralee's arm to force her to her feet. Pulling her close, Dante demanded, "Where is she?"

"I won't tell you."

Yanking her closer, he dropped his voice menacingly. "Where is she?"

"She's at Wolf Whistle Creek," Piper shouted, scared.

"Get on the horse," Dante commanded, and then he returned the rifle to the scabbard. He followed Lauralee up into the saddle.

"You," Dante said, looking at Piper. "Move ahead. Take us to Wolf Whistle Creek."

Piper caught Lauralee's eyes once and then kneed her mount forward.

"Stay near the tree line," Dante instructed.

They rode toward Fool's Peak and then cut westward to follow the trail to Wolf Whistle Creek. Piper sat stiffly, and Lauralee felt the weight of guilt for having dragged her friend into the middle of this situation. How hopelessly gullible she was to believe that Dante Quinn would turn himself in because Lauralee's father was in trouble. Dante Quinn had his own problems. Why would he care about her father?

As for Dante, he kept his arm around her middle. He never relaxed his grip. Perhaps he thought she would make a run for it if he loosened his arm. Maybe she would, but that wouldn't stop him from finding Emelina Istok and wouldn't help Wade Murphy if she ran home empty-handed.

After a long while, Dante asked in a low voice against her ear, "You hate me?"

"No."

He laughed softly as if he didn't believe her. "Sure you do. But for what it's worth, you're the first person I've trusted since I was a little boy. I'll leave after I see Emelina. You'll never see me again, and everything will turn right again for you."

She turned her head but couldn't see his face. "It won't turn right, Mr. Quinn. How will I ever make this up to my father?"

He straightened and his arm pulled her back against him. "Tell the sheriff that I held you at gunpoint. Your friend is witness."

"But Felton Ewing saw us together. He saw you kiss me."

"I'm a gypsy, Lauralee. Tell them I put you under a spell." When she didn't answer him, he continued. "You're young, and your friends will understand. They know you. They will forgive you."

Her shoulders sagged. "They know how stupidly fleeceable I am."

"You're not fleeceable," he told her. "You're trusting. I envy that. Trusting is one thing I will never be, and it is my curse more than the thieving."

"You can change."

"I'm not willing to change."

They rode on in silence after that. Half a mile northward, they came to a lane opening on their right. This they followed for a couple of miles as it climbed up and down into the country. Lauralee's heart sank further with every mile. Things would never be right with her father again. Emelina Istok had been right. Her union line was broken. Lauralee had a split in her family, and she would've never believed it possible, until today, when she saw the hurt in her father's face.

Water murmured. Foam glimmered where the stream flowed over a short fall. Suddenly, the trees came to an end, and the fog in the trees was left behind. Lauralee recognized the rounded wagons in the short distance, and she could see the man, Casamir, too. He did not sit whittling today but stood near a corral of horses. Though he'd acted standoffish yesterday, Lauralee remembered that he had kind eyes. She hoped he would be kind to Dante. This could perhaps be Dante's answer to his problems. He could live with the gypsies free from Shank and free of jail.

Two men stood with Casamir, and the rest of the families spread out between the wagons. It was early still, and the children seemed quieter than they had been yesterday afternoon. Lauralee didn't see Emelina among the people. It could be that she was inside one of the wagons.

A dog alerted the Roma people to the riders, and all activity ceased as the men and women turned to watch their approach. When their horses reached the pawpaw trees, Dante released Lauralee, dismounted, and walked toward the small gathering crowd.

Piper glanced at Lauralee. "Let's go," she whispered, but Lauralee shook her head. She slid from the horse and walked toward Dante. Piper remained in the saddle in the shade of the trees.

Dante took a breath for composure. "I'm here to speak to Emelina Istok." He saw the look of surprise cross several faces, as if they hadn't expected him to know her.

An older man stepped forward. "Who are you?"

"Is she here?"

"I asked who you are," the man said firmly. He spread his feet wide and his hands landed on the belt on his thick waist. He appeared to be fifty years old and wore a thick mustache.

A woman stepped forward from the group and stood by the

older man's side. Dante recognized her. She'd been at the street party in Omaha, the night he'd been beaten and cursed. Roza, he thought, remembering the old gypsy's words.

She considered him, and with a curled lip she announced, "He is *gaje!* He is not Roma."

"I am Emelina Istok's son."

A murmur surged through the group.

The older man stepped toward him. "My name is Casamir. Who are you, *chal?*"

"I am Dante Quinn."

Another man stepped forward. He was broad through the shoulders and wore only a vest and pants. His tanned stomach was muscled, and he stared at Dante with a look of challenge. "How do we know you are her son?" He stared at the older man. "We will send a runner, yes, Casamir, to our neighbor?" Turning to Dante again, he asked, "Which *natsia* do you belong?"

"I don't belong to a *natsia*. I was raised in San Francisco after Emelina left me."

"So you are half-stinking blood, *va?* Worse than *gaje*."

"Is Emelina here? I must speak to her." Dante felt his temper rising.

Casamir shook his head. "We cannot help you, Dante Quinn."

Roza smiled coyly. She stepped behind Dante and then circled to his left. "Make him prove that he is Roma, Casamir. Then we will tell him all about Emelina, *va?*"

The others laughed, but Casamir did not. "There is no reason for it."

"There is reason for it." Roza touched Dante's sleeve and then put her hand on his shoulder. "He claims to be Roma when I say he is not." She gazed to the men and women standing behind Casamir and spoke to them in their own language.

A cheer went up among them. Several children had joined the group, and they tittered in happy laughter.

Dante stepped away from Roza. "I will take your test, willingly."

Another cheer sounded from the crowd.

Casamir's dark eyes found Dante's and he stepped forward. In a low voice he said kindly, "You do not know what these tests are, *chal*. Are you sure you want to commit to them?" His large hand found Dante's shoulder. His bushy brows pulled together as he studied Dante's face.

"If I must prove myself to find Emelina, I will do it."

Roza clapped her hands and called loudly over the crowd. "Three tests to prove yourself, Dante Quinn." She circled in front of the crowd, encouraging them to cheer more.

Casamir nodded to Dante and stepped back toward the group.

"The first will be . . ." She gazed at the man who'd stepped forward previously, the one who'd called Dante half-blood. "Marko," Roza shouted, and the others clamored approval. "The one who remains standing is a true Roma."

The man Marko faced Dante and he stood taller, broader. His black hair was unwashed, and it lay thick and greasy against his head. Feathery brows arched atop his wide forehead. He smelled of sweat and horses, as if he'd just come from the pen.

Dante didn't have time to feint, the blow came so quickly. He landed in the leaves with blood gushing from his bottom lip.

The gypsies put their hands together loudly. Marko stepped forward, grabbed him by the front of his shirt, pulled Dante to his feet, and hit him in the gut.

Dante fell back with the blow.

Men called to Marko, encouraging him. Women taunted

Dante. He heard them call, "You will wash dishes with us to-night, pretty *gaje* man." Marko laughed along with them and circled like a champion in the ring, encouraging the crowd's reaction.

But stepping back with the blow helped Dante get his bearings. Marko was a thug, a street fighter. He had none of the finesse Dante was used to in his boxing matches at Creighton.

Marko came at him again, but Dante backed away, circled left to gain some of his strength, and then went into a semi-crouch with his fists up.

The men laughed, and Marko's face brightened. All seemed delighted that Dante meant to fight back.

Then Marko threw himself forward into his punch.

Dante slipped to the right and caught Marko in the ribs. Marko bent with the blow and favored that side when he lunged again.

Dante planted him with a right hook, pivoted on his left foot, and swung his right foot around.

Marko missed him like a bull missing a matador. He continued forward, unbalanced, and rammed headfirst into a tree. Rattled, Marko straightened. Red-eyed, he lunged again, swinging both fists.

Dante brought his elbows in tight to his body to reduce any damage the man's fists could inflict, and when Marko wasted the last of his energy, Dante gave him a quick straight punch in the nose. With his left fist, he brought in a semicircular punch to the side of the man's head.

Marko keeled into the dirt.

No one cheered after that. The men and women in the crowd stared at Dante, closemouthed, and waited for Roza to take charge again.

The beautiful gypsy sashayed forward to stand in front of

Dante. With a vixen smile, she touched his mouth with one finger. "Perhaps your blood is hotter than I first imagined." She turned her dark head toward the makeshift pen a small distance away from the wagons. "Do you see the wild mustangs?"

"Where did you find them?" Lauralee asked, staring at the horses. She'd come to stand beside Dante and held onto his arm.

"The horse is no match for the *Lowara* clan. They practically come to the men who want their strength and beauty. They are like women, *va,* the horses, with their hair and tempers." She turned her eyes to Dante. "You will tame the black horse. It is your second test." She spun away from him to kneel beside Marko, who was just coming around. She spoke to him softly, and he stared keenly at her as if listening to instructions.

Men and women followed Dante toward the corral while Lauralee stayed beside him. "Listen to me," she told him urgently. "You don't have to ride him to tame him. Separate him from the others. Don't make any sudden movements."

He could feel the beads of sweat breaking out on his forehead. "You mean, movements like running for my life?"

She gave him a quick grin, and Dante wondered for a moment why she stayed with him. Why hadn't she run off to find the chief or one of the deputies? But she was instructing him, and he tried to take in what she said.

"Show him your hands—approach him from the left side."

Confused, he asked, "His left or my left?"

Lauralee grabbed his elbow and forced him to look at her. "*His* left." Her smoke-blue eyes surveyed his chest and his waist. "Tuck in your shirt."

He jammed the shirt edge into his pants. His heart was racing, but he forced the fear into the background.

"To gain his trust, you must be firm but gentle. Talk quietly to him. Pet him."

"All right," he said with little breath.

"If he pushes you, push him back. Don't walk around him—make him walk around you."

His own legs felt loose and watery. "What if he walks *over* me?"

"He won't," she insisted. "He'll go around you, but if he gets near you, flap your arms. When he gets out of the way, praise him."

"Praise him for not killing me?"

"Finally, walk away from him. Make him follow you, Dante; lead him."

He stared at her. "Are you kidding?"

"For your sake, I hope you are a gypsy—and magical too. My father couldn't catch him and would've had a hard time breaking him if he did."

"Thanks for telling me that. I feel so much easier about it now."

"Sure," she said, as if she thought he meant it. "Once you can pat him, you win."

Roza stepped onto the bottom slat of the fence, as the other members of the clan stood scattered around the pen. She said in a loud voice, "If you are gypsy, you will be able to calm the horses, *va?* A true Roma could do it."

Dante stepped between the slats of the fence and faced the four horses. All of them followed the black stallion to the other side of the corral. He was the leader, obviously, and the one to tame. Dante took a step forward, knowing that the gypsies and Lauralee stood at the fence to watch. All remained quiet.

So quiet, in fact, that Dante heard his heart pounding in his ears. The sweat from his forehead trickled down the side of his face. He didn't wipe it. What had Lauralee told him to do? He couldn't remember one thing.

Stopping in the middle of the corral, he took a deep breath.

The black horse pranced forward ahead of the others. He was ready for this showdown and locked eyes with Dante. Tossing his head, he snorted and pranced forward.

Show him your hands . . .

Dante held out his palms, sweaty and hot.

The horse snorted again, pushed his front hooves into the dirt, and galloped to the right. The other horses followed him round the pen as if they meant to stampede.

He won't run over you, Lauralee had told him. How could Dante trust that information? He glanced at Lauralee and saw her concern for him. Her lovely face showed the stress of the situation. Her eyes screwed up in the sun and it looked as if she might cry.

But Dante trusted Lauralee. He might regret it later, but he trusted her in this matter.

The lead horse passed on his left, and Dante stepped right into the path of the other horses. The second horse veered right with the other two following it. They went to a different corner of the corral, whinnying in fright.

What had Lauralee told him? *Separate him from the others.*

Dante was doing this all backward. Still, the horse was separated from the group, no matter how it had happened. With palms out he walked toward the black stallion, approaching from the left side of the horse. Slowly he moved forward.

Talk quietly to him.

Well, what do you say to a horse anyway? "Good . . . good boy," he said softly and clicked his tongue. "You're a good one, you are."

The stallion snorted and shifted left to right.

Dante moved forward again and caught the horse's stare. Relaxing his shoulders, he dropped his voice further. "You're a fine horse, a good horse. We'll be friends, you and I. You're a fine boy."

The horse snorted and trotted left.

Dante moved with him, cutting off his exit.

Just as Lauralee said, the horse didn't touch him, but moved to the right. Still cornered, the stallion snorted again and whinnied.

"Calm down. We're going to be friends."

It was an odd look the stallion gave him while bobbing his head up and down.

With locked eyes, Dante suddenly understood the stallion. He didn't trust anyone, just as Dante didn't trust anyone.

"We're alike, you and I," he told the horse calmly, confidently. He took another few steps forward. "I know how you feel and I won't hurt you. You can trust me."

The horse settled a little and backed away from Dante's approach. Dante took another step and reached out his hand. *Steady.* Would the stallion rear and kick? Somehow Dante didn't think so. An invisible blanket of peace settled over his shoulders, and he felt his breathing slow. And it was the oddest thing to see, but the black chest of the beast slowed in rhythm too. The horse was calming down. Dante touched its neck. "Good boy. Good boy. You're a good one, you are."

The horse whinnied in return and let Dante pat him. Loud murmurings came from behind him as the gypsies spoke one to another. They bobbed their heads and cast approving looks at Dante. With one last pat, he walked toward the fence to Lauralee. The stallion followed him.

She said, "You obviously have a lot of gypsy blood in you, sir. That was impressive."

"Was it?" He slipped through the slats to stand beside her and the red-haired young woman named Piper.

"I've never seen anyone tame a horse so quickly," Piper told him. "Especially one so temperamental. Look at him now."

Dante turned and watched as three men approached the horse that reared and kicked its hooves. He gazed at Lauralee. "They don't have the magic, I guess."

To his left, Roza stepped toward him. "Very good, Dante Quinn. There is only one thing left for you to do."

"And then you will tell me what I want to know," he said sharply, his muscles tensing.

She smiled wickedly. "You must pass the third test."

The group, led by Casamir now, moved toward the wagons where, once there, everyone sat in a circle. Remains of a fire faded in the middle of the ring, where Dante stood with Roza. Lauralee and Piper stood outside the circle to watch them. Another Roma woman stepped through the circle and handed Roza a cup filled with liquid.

Roza lifted the cup in front of Dante but did not give it to him. She spoke loudly. "You will drink the gypsy cup. If you are gypsy, you will live. If you are not . . ."

She circle behind him with the cup still held high. "Three hearts of precious wild pink rose that under the sun and starlight grows. Three silver spoons of honey . . . three silver spoons of brandy wine." She stood in front of Dante again and handed him the cup. "Drink."

"Why should I? I've proved to you that I am Roma. I am Emelina Istok's son. This is foolishness."

She shrugged her shoulders. "Perhaps you *are* Roma, but if you want to know about Emelina, you will drink the cup."

"What is it?"

"A mixture of ingredients to bring out the proof of your blood."

Her answer made him angry. All his life he'd tried to prove

he *wasn't* a gypsy. Now, to get the answers he craved, he had to prove what he hated most about himself. Putting the rim of the cup to his lips, Dante drank the entire contents of it. It smelled heady and tasted like thick and bitter wine. When he'd finished, he pushed the cup at the gypsy woman.

He felt nothing, and he smiled triumphantly at her. "There. Are you happy?"

Roza's face went out of focus for a moment. Dante closed his eyes and tried to see her clearly. His thoughts came fast and he began to sweat again. A hard lump formed in his stomach. At first it merely annoyed him, but suddenly it caught at him, and Dante bent over. Sweat beaded again. He felt so hot, all over.

Roza touched his shoulders. When he peered into her face, he saw that she smiled. And then Lauralee was there, holding on to him. She asked above his head, "What have you done?"

"The drink knows if he is Roma or not."

"What if he isn't?"

"He dies."

On his knees now, Dante held tightly to Lauralee's arm. "But he's only half Roma." She asked the gypsy, "What will happen?"

"If he lives, he will be completely Roma. There will be no *gaje* left in him."

It was the last thing Dante heard before all went black.

Chapter Ten

Lauralee sat beside Dante on the ground after he'd passed out. His breath was so shallow it scared her. She needed to find a way to get him to Uncle Todd's office, but she didn't know how to do that. He could die before they reached town. "What can we do?" she asked Piper, who kneeled beside her.

"I could ride to town and bring Dr. Thomas here."

"No, we need to take him there and do it now." She stared at the men in the circle and caught Casamir's eyes. Lauralee got to her feet. "Please help me. I have to take him to the doctor. Will you help me get him onto a horse?"

"He took the drink on his own," Casamir told her softly. He stepped forward. "No doctor will be able to help him, *chav*."

"*Fah!*"

Lauralee spun around at the word and saw Roza bent toward Dante Quinn, watching him closely. A queer light burned in her eyes. She said, "Your *gaje* doctor will not know what to do. Quinn will live or die on his own."

Lauralee's jaw hurt, she clenched her teeth so tightly. Stepping forward, she bent to face the beautiful woman. "You

147

poisoned him, didn't you? You don't want him to be gypsy be- cause he's only half-blood."

Roza sneered at her. "You know nothing of our ways . . ."

Dante groaned and took a long, deep breath.

She let out a laugh. "You see? No need to take him away. He is Roma." She straightened and lifted her hands to those still sitting in the circle. "He is Roma."

Applause sounded and people got to their feet, but Lauralee continued to kneel beside Dante. When his eyes fluttered open, she searched his face. "Are you all right?"

"What happened?" he asked, closing his eyes again.

"You passed out."

Roza knelt next to him again. "You did well, Dante Quinn. You have proved you are Roma. We are one now. You will stay here with us."

Her last words provoked hot jealousy in Lauralee's heart. "He doesn't have to stay here."

Roza didn't look at her, didn't seem to think Lauralee mat- tered in the least. She told Dante, "I have been wrong about you, and for this I must seek an answer from the *drúkkerébema.*" She placed her hand on his chest. "You have much passion. And you are different since I met you, Dante Quinn. It is proof that you need to leave the *gaje.* A Roma cannot be happy with the *gaje.*" She leaned forward, and her black curls fell about her. Dante's eyes held hers. "You will find happiness here."

Dante pushed to his elbows, staring hard at the woman. "I want to speak to Emelina Istok."

Roza shook her head. She had not moved away when Dante tried to sit forward. Her face stayed near to his. "You cannot speak to Emelina Istok, Dante."

"Why not?"

"She is dead."

"What?" He came off the ground in a hurry. Roza and Laura-lee followed suit and stood with him in the middle of the circle. His voice sounded shaky, heated. "She cannot be dead. I have to speak to her. It is urgent."

"The wild man in the hills killed her," Roza explained. "He killed your mother."

Lauralee stepped toward them. "Levi?"

The gypsy woman at last turned toward Lauralee. "Levi, yes. Levi Bloodcrow. He killed Emelina Istok."

"No, I don't believe you," Dante said, backing away from them. "That cannot be true."

"*Viata de apoi.* She is in the afterlife, *va?*" Roza reached for him, touching his sleeve.

Dante wrenched away from her. "I don't believe you."

"It is the truth, whether you choose to believe it or not. *Gilo;* she has departed."

His shoulders sagged with her words, as if he accepted them. Staring at the women, he shook his head. *"Damnation!"* Spinning from them, Dante walked out of the circle.

Dead? She is dead. How very inconvenient, he thought stupidly, but in life and death the woman had let him down. Dante breathed heavily as his stomach roiled again. He made it to a slender tree and vomited near the stream. Roza had surely poisoned him with the drink . . . and it didn't matter. He didn't care. Leaning on the tree, he skidded down the bark into a sitting position.

What was left for him, Dante wondered, staring at the water and the pebbles beneath it. What was left was no answers and jail time. And he didn't care. All his feelings, his obsessions, his ardor, and his drive had been pulled out of him with the gypsy's words.

Now he was full-fledged gypsy. He could stay with them. Live here. At least he would be free. But once he began stealing from them, they would kick him out, and he would be in the same predicament.

How had it all come to this? Two weeks ago he was at Creighton, enjoying his schoolwork and looking forward to his job in California. Now he sat near his own vomit, a broken man. A Roma by trial and by witness. One hundred percent gypsy.

Ipso facto.

And there was only one thing left to do.

"You cannot leave," Roza told Dante. The desperation in her voice caught a sympathetic chord in Lauralee. "You belong with us. You belong to *me.*"

"I belong to no one," Dante said flatly. He didn't look at the woman when he said it, and neither did he look at Lauralee.

"You will never be happy outside the clan."

"I may not be happy, but I must go." He walked toward the pawpaw trees where the horses stood. Piper waited for them, staring wide-eyed and gripping the horn of the saddle as if she meant to mount quickly and gallop off. Surely when Lauralee woke her this morning, Piper had had no idea what this day would hold.

Roza followed Dante. "Why? Why do you feel you must leave?"

Dante turned his dark eyes on Lauralee and she held her breath. He said, "I owe her a great deal. She risked much to help me, and I need to return the favor. I will go with her and help her father."

Lauralee's heart began its rhythm again. Maybe everything

would turn out all right after all. If Dante told Shank about his sleepwalking and stealing, Shank might grant him leniency.

"You cannot leave," Roza said with more urgency and a hint of anger. She grabbed Dante's arm to make him stop. "You drank the cup."

His thick brows pulled together. "I can leave and I will."

"Marko!" she screamed, and the man who'd fought Dante rushed to Roza's side. She spoke to him in the Roma language, and he blanched at her words. He returned her fervor, but in English, at least two English words that Lauralee recognized: *love potion.*

"You gave him a love potion?" Lauralee asked, her chest tight with fury. "It wasn't a test then. You're trying to make him stay against his will."

Roza paled in the high sunshine. "It was not a love potion. It was the ceremonial drink. You are gypsy," she told Dante. "You survived."

Dante glanced at Lauralee. "Let's go."

"Wait," Lauralee said, turning to Roza. "Is there any way to cure a curse of thievery?"

Roza's mouth was straight in anger, but she answered the question. "I know of no curse for thievery."

"But how do you get rid of a curse? Surely there is a way to do it."

Her face drained of emotion, and Lauralee didn't think she would answer, but she did. In a flat voice, she said, "Only the one who cast the spell can remove the curse."

Piper was already on her horse, and Lauralee climbed on behind her. Dante rode before them, leading the way toward Fool's Peak and toward the Martin River, where they had found him that morning.

Lauralee felt Dante's anguish as acutely as if it had been

her own disappointment. It seemed there was no finality to his problems. He belonged nowhere: not to the gypsies, not to a family, and not to Lauralee.

But what a foolish thought. She couldn't be with Dante. She couldn't fall in love with him. He was a felon, a fugitive, and that made him very bad husband material. Yet the way that Roza had looked at him had made Lauralee feel such jealousy that she could barely breathe.

And the witch had tried to sneak him a love potion.

Lauralee wondered why he hadn't been affected by it. Didn't that prove that the gypsy curses were nonsense? If it did, then Dante stole things without being cursed. That made him guilty.

Roza had been correct, however, when she claimed that Dante Quinn had changed. He'd been a cold character when Lauralee first met him too, but how he'd burned with passion in his quest for Emelina. He made a fine horseman, after all, and quite the boxer, too. It had all been quite thrilling, and all for naught: Emelina was dead.

What a curious thing that was, Lauralee thought. Emelina must've died yesterday, but why was she out in the foothills?

Someone had to have taken her there and witnessed her death. Had the gypsies banished her to her fate? Casamir certainly had not been happy to see her, and Roza didn't seem to care for the old woman either. Still, what an awful fate it was, to be torn to bits by Levi Bloodcrow. How could anyone condone that?

It was well past noon when they rode out of the trees. Traveling quietly, Dante directed his horse farther up a slope and stayed near the tree line. Dismounting, he ducked beneath a low branch and then stood in the gravel near a boulder. Piper and Lauralee dismounted too and stood beside him. Their view was of the valley floor with pines poking toward the azure sky. "What's wrong?" Lauralee asked Dante.

"I saw Emelina."

"What? But she's—"

"Ahead of us on the lane," he interrupted her. Though he spoke softly, his tone was insistent. "She was in a buggy. Her gray hair . . . I saw her gray hair."

Lauralee watched the valley floor but saw nothing.

Dante twisted around to look at her. "They lied." He moved quickly downhill toward the horses.

Piper started to follow him, but Lauralee touched her arm. "He gazed toward Fool's Peak," Lauralee whispered.

Her friend's reaction was what she expected. She backed away from Lauralee and shook her head. "I don't want to go there. Levi . . ."

"I don't want you to go there. I want you to find my father— or Rick. Tell them where I am."

"You're not going . . . ?" Her green eyes were glassy, as if she were about to cry.

Lauralee glanced at Dante. "Something's wrong with him. Whatever they gave him to drink has affected him somehow. I didn't see a buggy, did you?"

"No. Lauralee, I'm scared. I don't want you to go with him."

"I'll be all right, but find my father. Go. I'll ride with Dante," she said, and she walked with Piper toward the horses. "I'll make an excuse." She broke loose of Piper's arm and walked quickly downhill toward Dante. He'd already swung his leg over the saddle and grabbed the reins.

"May I ride with you?" Lauralee asked, standing near his leg and gazing at him while shading her eyes from the sun with her fingers. "Our horse is acting tired."

Dante held out his hand and she took it. Settled behind him, Lauralee glanced at Piper. "Hurry," she told her.

They rode through the valley and then moved upslope, where the trees thinned and the rocks became boulders. Fool's Peak loomed before them. They hadn't caught up with Emelina—or whoever it was whom Dante thought he saw, but it was not for want of speed. Dante pushed the horse to a full gallop. When they neared the peak, he reined in and told Lauralee to dismount. He followed her down.

Perhaps because of her last experience in this spot, Lauralee knew uneasiness. With every sigh of the wind and every creak of a branch, she whipped around, expecting Levi to charge them. Dante went toward the edge of the cliff and looked at the rocks below. Lauralee scooted along to stay near him.

His dark eyes found hers once, and then he glanced behind her. "Where is she? Where is your friend?"

Without looking at him, because in the wind shadows moved in the trees, she whispered her reply. "She was too scared to come along. She's scared of Levi. So am I."

His hands found her elbows, and he whipped Lauralee around to face him. Whispering too, he said, accusingly, "You told her to hurry. That was the last thing you said to her. Why? You sent her to get the chief and his deputies, didn't you?"

She stared back at him. "I told her to find my papa or my brother."

"When I'm about to find Emelina, you call for help?"

"Emelina's dead."

"She lied. Roza lied."

"Maybe you're seeing things, Dante. Whatever she gave you has made you sick. Maybe you're hallucinating."

"I saw her," he ground out, releasing Lauralee roughly. He shook his head. "I'm so stupid. I thought I could trust you.

Well, that's what I get, isn't it, for trusting a woman? This is incredible."

She tried to make him look at her. She stepped around him when he faced the rocks again. "I've helped you as much as I can. It's gone too far. Others are getting hurt. You're hurt. Uncle Todd should look at you."

"Who is getting hurt?"

"My father!"

He was white about the nostrils. "I saw her—"

"Hello?" a man's voice said, reverberating in the rocks all around them. "Hello?"

Dante grabbed Lauralee and pulled her behind the boulder with him. They hunkered in the fist-sized gravel. "It's Levi," Lauralee hissed, wide-eyed. "He's coming for us."

Dante held up his hand to silence her. He moved around the boulder and peeked over the shelf of rocks below them. "It's Emelina."

"It is not Emelina—"

"Look for yourself."

Lauralee waddled to squat next to him. It *was* Emelina. She stood next to Oliver Beckett, who cupped his mouth and called out again, "Hello?"

"Does he know we're here?" Lauralee asked, staying close to Dante. He started to stand, but she kept her hand on his arm. "What do you think you're doing?"

"I'm going to go talk to her."

"Wait, no. Let me go first." She pulled his arm hard to make him listen. "You'll only scare her. Let me talk to her."

"Why? What good will that do?"

She bit her lip and looked at Oliver beneath her. "I have an idea. Something's not right here, Dante."

He brushed her hand away. "I'll go."

"Wait . . . she's scared of you, Dante, and she's not going to help you. If you go down there gangbusters, she'll curse you again with something worse. Trust me, like you did before. You can come out whenever you want, but give me a few minutes."

She walked away from him without waiting for his reply. Climbing down the slope, she stepped onto the lane where a day carriage sat.

They heard her coming, and Oliver Beckett turned her way first.

"You . . . ?" Emelina asked. Her gray eyes screwed up at the corners, and her thin lips parted. She wore the same purple skirt and dingy blouse. Her wristbands caught the high sun and glinted with it. The ruby that hung around her neck looked blood red against her skin.

"Hello again," Lauralee greeted, using a friendly tone and waving as she approached. Then she saw who sat in the carriage, and she stopped walking.

Esme Beckett stepped out of the buggy. "Lauralee, what are you doing here, dear? You shouldn't have come." She wore her black shawl, and her dark hair fell onto it.

Ignoring Esme, Lauralee turned toward the gypsy. "I need to speak to you. Please. I saw you crossing the valley, and I followed you."

The old woman didn't like that. Her gray eyes narrowed and her voice, strong in tone, sharpened. "You followed me?"

"Yes." She walked to stand in front of the woman, ignoring both Esme and Oliver. "I must ask you something." She glanced at the Becketts.

Esme stood beside Oliver now. She reached out for Lauralee's hand as if she meant to pull her away from Emelina.

Lauralee stepped away and moved around the gypsy so that

she faced all three of them together. She asked Emelina, "You said I have *kpache,* remember?"

With the two women standing side by side, Lauralee realized how much Esme and Emelina looked alike. They weren't only related; they were close relatives—sisters, perhaps, although Esme looked younger. Lauralee eyed the gypsy again. "I wonder if you could help me put a curse on someone."

Emelina smiled wickedly, disbelief marked her features. "You want to learn to curse someone?"

"Yes."

"You are not Roma," the old woman answered. "You cannot curse people. Only *Kalderasha* use the curse."

"All right," Lauralee conceded, wondering where Dante stood. Had he followed her, or did he watch from above them still? "Will you tell me how to remove a curse?"

"You've been cursed?" Emelina asked. It seemed the prospect delighted her. Her thin lips split. Lauralee saw her brown-stained teeth. "How have you been cursed?"

"I steal things . . ."

Esme gasped. "Lauralee?"

"Can you help me?" Lauralee pleaded to the gypsy. "I'm in trouble and I need you to help me."

"No," Emelina told her. "You are not cursed. You are lying and you are stupid, *va?*"

"But you have to help me. Please."

Emelina's jaw jutted forward. "Who cursed you?"

"Emelina Istok."

The words had the desired affect, but from Esme first. "How do you know Emelina, Lauralee?"

"Is she dead?"

Oliver answered. He stepped away from his mother. Still wearing his maroon work vest, he faced Lauralee. His black hair was curled tightly on top of his head. "Who have you been talking to, Lauralee? Where did you hear about Emelina Istok?"

"What do you know about her, Oliver?" Lauralee asked him in return.

Dante Quinn stood beside her suddenly. He stepped toward Oliver Beckett. "You told me you never saw her."

Oliver squared himself up. He wasn't as tall as Dante, but he was thicker through the chest and arms. They had the same black hair. Oliver's was much more wavy and out of control. "I saw her all right. I watched her die."

Chapter Eleven

Why did everyone believe she was dead? Emelina stood right there in front of them. Dante's ears rang in confusion. Surely he wasn't the only person who could see her. He aimed a finger at the gypsy. "She's right here."

The woman standing next to Lauralee stepped toward Dante. "Who are you?" she asked gently while watching him with her dark, dark eyes. She looked familiar, and the impression that hit him was one of a distant sweetness and remembrance of a different time.

"Dante Quinn."

The woman covered her mouth with cupped fingers. "—Dante?" Tears filled her eyes until they pooled onto her lashes. "Oh, my boy, my dear young man." She reached for his hand. "I am your aunt, Esme." She stepped closer to him, searching his eyes with her own. Her hand on his felt warm and strong. "But your mama is dead. You know that."

He closed his eyes and took deep breaths, trying to push his anger back down. Pulling his hand away, he jammed a finger at Emelina again. "She's not dead. She *left* me." His passion nearly blinded him, and Esme Beckett blurred in front of him. "Emelina left me."

"Your mother would never have left you," the woman said softly. "She loved you, Dante."

"What are you talking about?" Stepping away, he glared at his mother again. "You left me when I was six years old. Do you think I can't remember?"

Something dark flickered through his mother's dark eyes, and she turned her face slightly away from him. Disdain scored her mouth. Dante stepped toward her. "I recognized you, and that's why you ran from me. I said your name and you bolted. . . ."

"I'll bet she did," said another voice behind him. Turning, he saw the railroad station worker, Beckett, standing beside Lauralee. A sneer of contempt touched his mouth—but then Esme caught Dante's attention again as she moved between him and Emelina. Esme was taller than his mother, more square shouldered and proud. She swept her hand toward the gypsy. "This isn't your mama, Dante. This is your Aunt Ophelia." She caught his eyes and held them. "Your mother died."

Anger stirred higher in his chest. "I don't believe you." His ears no longer rang, and every sound seemed to intensify suddenly. The scrape of Beckett's boot in the dirt, Esme's shortness of breath, the footsteps in the woods to his left . . . he could hear it all.

"Listen to me, cousin," Beckett said, seizing Dante's attention. "I was there. I saw what happened to your mother." He stared angrily at the gypsy—at Ophelia, as Esme called her.

"Stop," the gypsy hissed. "Or you will die too."

Beckett scoffed and turned away from her. "When I was fifteen, I ran from my home. I ran because Ophelia told me that I was Roma, that I was missing a carefree life." His nostrils flared with his heated memory. "She told me I was gypsy because my parents wouldn't give her any more money to keep silent about it."

"Oliver . . . ," Esme warned, taking his arm.

"No, Mama, I won't be quiet about it anymore." His dark eyes flashed at Dante again. "My mother hid the truth from me too. She tells people we are Spanish."

Esme Beckett glanced at Lauralee over her shoulder as if she was embarrassed about the truth even now. A tinge of pink touched her high cheekbones.

Oliver kept on. "I followed Ophelia and my real father to San Francisco. They met your mama there, cousin. They wanted her to pay."

Dante's mouth felt so stiff he barely got out the words. "Pay for what?"

"Silence. She paid for secrecy." His hand tightened on Dante's shoulder. "They blackmailed her, just as they did my mother. They threatened to tell everyone that you were a gypsy boy." He tilted his head to challenge, "What sort of bigotry do you think your great father would face if his friends and colleagues knew he'd married a gypsy and fathered a black-eyed child with a wandering spirit, eh?"

The question stunned him. Lack of breath caused a deep ache in Dante's chest. Obviously, his father knew nothing about the blackmail. He would've stopped it. He would've brought charges against the gypsies. But he couldn't have known. He'd thought his wife left him for her old life. Dante had thought she'd left him . . .

Beckett pressed further. "When your mama couldn't sneak money to them any longer, they demanded something else from her. They wanted the red emerald your mother wore around her neck."

"The red . . ." The memory of the jewel flashed in Dante's

mind. It was what had attracted him at the street carnival in Omaha. The red emerald belonged to his father. He'd given it to Emelina as a wedding gift. It had been a family keepsake . . . Dante stared at the gypsy's leathery neck and at the jewel dangling there.

"That's right. You remember, don't you?" Oliver encouraged. "But how much do you recall, I wonder." He shoved Dante's shoulder hard. "Let me help you. You were a little boy, no more than first grade, I think, and you were on your way home from school, walking up the slope to your house."

Dante focused on Beckett. What was he talking about, a memory—an old, old memory?

"I saw you myself from the alley where I hid with Ophelia. We watched as a man approached you and you stupidly stopped to listen to him. He wanted to show you a red emerald."

In a moment, Dante transferred back to that overcast day on the sidewalk. Seagulls piped overhead, and the ocean roared in the not-too-distant background. A man indeed had stopped him. A giant of a man, and Dante had felt as though he couldn't run. He was too small. The man touched his shoulder, just as Beckett touched it now, and he held out his hand with a stone resting on top of it. "I'd only ever seen one like it. They are extremely rare," Dante recalled aloud. "My mother wore a red emerald . . ."

"The one he showed you *was* your mother's stone. The man stopped you to prove to Emelina that he could get to you if he wanted to; it was his way of trying to get more money from her. When Emelina found out, she attacked him."

"Attacked who?" Dante wanted to know, rage growing inside him. "Who was he?"

Oliver nodded toward Ophelia and to the trees behind her. "Him."

An enormous man stepped out of the trees. Dante knew instantly that he'd been the one moving through the woods on the left. He'd been biding his time, apparently, until the gypsy waved him forward. Feral and filthy, he was the same half-animal who'd attacked Lauralee last week. He snarled at Dante, and then at Beckett, his lip curling beneath his fetid beard.

Beckett turned loose of him and swung his arm toward the wild man. "Dante, meet my father, Levi Bloodcrow."

Fear tightened painfully in her chest, and Lauralee's back hit the rock wall. Levi . . . Her mind scampered like a monkey through the pines. Levi Bloodcrow. The gypsy woman Roza had said the name. She'd been the first to proclaim that Levi Bloodcrow had killed Dante's mother. So it was true. Emelina was dead, and Dante had chased Ophelia through several states, thinking he'd found his mother. And now Ophelia meant to kill them all by pointing Levi Bloodcrow at them. But why did he live in the woods like an animal? Had he gone mad after he'd killed Emelina? Yet the most irrational accusation of all was that this wild man, this gargantuan gorilla of a gypsy, with his blistered face and filthy hair, was Oliver Beckett's father.

Inching along the rocks and ready to bolt, something else caught Lauralee's eyes. Riders on horseback galloped toward the peak. She let out a sob and pushed herself off the wall. The riders were still far enough off that she couldn't tell who they were, but, oh, how she hoped one was her father. Then she heard the old gypsy woman's voice, and Lauralee felt herself freeze.

"Churi dinili, rat, Chingary meripen," Ophelia chanted in a voice that scratched like an out-of-tune violin.

"No!" Esme screamed, putting out a hand to stop the flow of words. "No, you cannot do this!"

Ophelia laughed and then scowled at her sister. "You shame

us, you and Emelina, marrying *gaje,* mixing blood, and threat-
ening the *Kalderasha* spirit. You threaten the purity of my
kpashe. You and Emelina are dead to me." She pointed her
crooked finger at Dante. "This mixed blood will die with you,
and the spirits will return to me again." She twisted toward
Levi Bloodcrow. *"Churi dinnilli."* She pulled the necklace off
her skin and dangled it before him. *"Belneme."*

"This is why you brought us here, isn't it? You lied to us, just
as you always have . . ." Esme faced Levi Bloodcrow. "She is
lying to you. She will not reward you."

Lauralee watched as Levi swung around to snarl at Esme.
He stepped forward, but then he stopped and a strange expression crossed his features. Apparently, somewhere in his troubled mind, he recognized her.

Esme pulled back her shoulders and stuck out her chin.
"Levi Bloodcrow, you will not harm our son." Her voice was a
cold, clear bell. "I forbid it. He is your flesh and blood. Do
you not remember?"

The wild man winced at her words as if the truth of them
scored his flesh. He took a step forward and then raised his
hands as if to strike her.

"Do you not remember me?" Esme spoke softer, but just as
boldly. "Do you not remember that we once loved each other?"

Different emotions crossed the man's blistered face. He
stepped toward her, but suddenly spun around to face the gypsy.

"Chingary," Ophelia raged at him. *"Chingary."*

Bloodcrow twisted toward Esme, appearing more insane
than ever. He pulled back his arm to strike her.

Oliver jumped in front of his mother. Dante went into a
crouched position with his fists balled. He too stepped in front
of Esme.

Ophelia sneered at their courage and let out a bark of witch-like laughter. "You will both die, but you, Dante Quinn, your *gaje* blood stinks. You think to find me, chase me with your questions. Well, you will have your answers . . . Levi."

With a powerful blow, Levi Bloodcrow belted Oliver in the mouth. Beckett flew backward and struck the rock wall hard. Esme let out a scream and fell to her knees beside her son. Bloodcrow merely glanced at them and turned to face Dante Quinn.

The rage inside Dante pushed higher, tingeing his voice with a furious growl. "You killed my mother? You killed a woman who protected her child?"

"Show him," the old gypsy cackled on Dante's left. "Show him how you killed Emelina Quinn."

From the back of his tattered waistband, Levi drew out a dagger. The blade of it winked in the sunshine. He gripped it hard in his hand by the hilt and took a step forward. "Do you know me?" he asked Dante with a voice as abrasive as sandpaper. "Do you remember me, boy?"

Dante felt no fear, only fury. "Yes, I remember well. I should've killed you then."

"You kill me?" Levi asked, his laugh rat-a-tatting like bullets from a rifle. "You think you can kill me just as she thought she could." He held up the blade. "She tried to stab me with this knife, this one. She tried to kill me, but I dug it into her instead. I watched her soul fade away in her eyes. They were dark like yours, and I will watch you fade away too."

Wrath exploded inside of him. Screaming in rage, Dante flung himself at Bloodcrow before the man had a chance to bring the knife down.

A rifle shot split the air.

Neither man released his grip on the other. Levi pulled back on the blade to plunge it toward Dante's chest, but Dante caught his arm. Levi barred down. He was strong, but Dante locked his muscles. Digging his boots into the dirt, he held his ground. Levi pushed hard. The knife inched toward Dante's chest. Relaxing his grip, Dante bent his knees, swung around, and twisted Levi's arm backward . . . The knife plunged deep into Levi's chest.

A great gasp of air shot out of Levi's mouth, and he bent with the force of the blade. He stumbled backward, caught his boot on the side of a boulder, and fell.

Dante fell too, against the rock wall, and stared at Levi as a great sadness came over him. Not because the man was dead; Dante wanted him dead. The sadness was for his mother and the way that she had died.

Fourteen riders burst into the clearing, rifles drawn and pointed at the men. Chief Shank swung off his horse first and approached Dante Quinn. And then Lauralee saw her father and ran into his arms. Relief blanketed her—and shame. "Please forgive me," she pleaded. "I'm so sorry. I never meant to hurt you." She clung to his shirt.

Her father gripped her shoulders and held her at arm's length. "I don't care about it, Lauralee," he told her in a thick voice. "I don't care about anything as long as you're safe."

"But I sabotaged your chances . . ."

"I don't care," he said again, pulling her to him. "I wanted to be governor, but I'd rather have my daughter safe and whole." He pulled her closer and kissed the top of her head. "It will all work out fine. It'll be fine now," he told her when she continued to cry on his shirt.

Suddenly, she pulled away from him with her nose running and tears still streaming. "I swear I won't be gullible anymore. I'll question things and I'll think them through." When he laughed at her, Lauralee took hold of his shirt in her fists. "I mean it. I will be wise and thoughtful. Wait and see."

"I believe you," he said somberly, and then he grinned at her. Tucking her beneath his arm, they turned to watch Chief Shank and his men approach Dante Quinn, weapons drawn.

Dante continued to stare at the fallen man, who was lying bent and dead on the ground in front of him. Blood pooled beneath his body and circled onto the ground. And all of Dante's craze and passion flowed out too. He was nothing but a hollow shell leaning against the rock wall. Nothing mattered anymore. He deserved whatever he got, whether it was festering in a jail cell for the rest of his life, or whatever other punishment the court decided to mete out.

And then Dante remembered his studies. *Shaughn Danner, Esq. vs. Bartholomew Marquette,* Lincoln County, 1896. Marquette, accused of killing Danner's wife, was sentenced to death by hanging after Danner obsessively pursued him and brought him to justice. After the execution, Danner took a chair and set it next to his wife's tombstone, and he sat there until he died, eleven months later.

A shadow drifted over Levi Bloodcrow's body, and then it slid toward him. It was Chief Shank. He put his hand on Dante's shoulder. "You're under arrest, Mr. Quinn."

"It was self-defense," Lauralee insisted, stepping away from her father. "Levi attacked him with a knife. Surely you saw what happened?"

"It will all be considered, but he's still under arrest for burglary and running from the law." He pulled a pair of cuffs from his belt and held them out. "And for letting me bust down a door to see a half-naked woman rinsing out her unmentionables in a basin." Behind him were the deputies who had hunted for Dante at the hotel. They'd both dismounted. Still on her horse was Piper.

The chief glanced to his left and instructed in a sharp tone, "Ma'am, I want you to stay right where you are." He spoke to Ophelia Istok, who had turned toward the trees; it seemed she meant to slip away.

"She told Levi to kill them," Lauralee put in. "And Levi meant to do it, but Dante stopped him."

When every eye turned on her, Ophelia said, "I will not be arrested by the *gaje*. My *natsia* will judge me. They will speak the judgment."

Chief Shank looked at Esme Beckett. She kneeled beside Oliver, who sat in the dirt rubbing his head. "Is Lauralee telling the truth?" Shank wanted to know. "Did Levi try to hurt you?"

Esme nodded. "Yes, but please, will someone help my son? He's hurt. Levi struck Oliver, and he hit his head against the rocks."

Wade Murphy and Deputy Vaughn helped Oliver into the carriage. Esme climbed into the back to sit beside him. Deputy Casillo stood over Levi's hulking frame and told the chief, "He's dead all right. You want me and Vaughn to bury him?"

"No, we'll take him with us and give him to the undertaker. That'll give Charlie something to do for a change." Placing the cuffs on Dante's wrist, Shank led him toward the horses. "But let's do this quickly. We've got to get our fugitive to town and take depositions from everyone else. You," he said, pointing to Ophelia. "You'll come with us."

She rode double with Piper and sat in front of her in the saddle. Piper asked, "Are you all right?"

Lauralee shrugged. Her hands still trembled. She hadn't

eaten, and after watching Levi die, she thought she might never eat again. More than that, however, she was concerned about Dante. What would become of him?

Turning her head, Lauralee meant to ease Piper's anxiety and said, "You found everyone very quickly. You saved the day, Calamity Jane."

"That's true," Piper admitted. "But Prince here"—she patted the horse's rump—"understood there was trouble. We flew across the valley and luckily saw the posse riding toward Fool's Peak."

"I'm surprised you followed, with your fear of the place."

"She's very brave," a male voice put in. It was Deputy Efren Vaughn. He'd maneuvered his horse to trot near Laura- lee's mount. He didn't acknowledge her, but instead he smiled sweetly at Piper.

As if she weren't already nauseous enough!

And then the most appalling thing happened. Piper giggled, *giggled* at the man. There it was, Lauralee's cue to retch.

It seemed the entire town turned out to see the cat burglar arrested. The posse and prisoners came into Victor City on the west road and circled around to cross the Naberling Bridge and then halted in front of the police station. By the time they stopped, at least a hundred people stood in the wide road. Big Buck and Billy Yank watched from the alleyway, and Axel Garvey leaned against the hitching posts. Others stood on the walkway and in front of the stores.

Getting off her horse, Lauralee remained between Wade Mur- phy and Piper. Chief Shank called out, "Someone get Doc Todd over here." He walked toward the horse he'd been leading, and after Dante dismounted, the chief took him by the arm. They hadn't taken two steps when a blur of dark gray and white fur flashed across the road. The monkey jumped toward Dante and then climbed into his arms. With his hands cuffed, Dante could do little but stare at the animal in surprise.

It was a golden necklace that the monkey stuffed into Dante's shirt pocket, and then it let out a chattering wail that caused everyone to take a large step backward. "Hey," Buck said, stepping forward. "What's this all about? You using my monkey to steal jewelry?"

The animal chattered wildly at Buck and flung his arms around Dante's neck.

"So that's how you did it," Efren Vaughn said, standing beside Piper. "You had your pet monkey robbing the town and bringing you the loot."

Dante shook his head. "I never met this monkey before in my life."

Esme stepped out of the carriage then and stood beside Dante Quinn. "That's because it's not your pet. It's hers," she said, pointing to Ophelia, who was still sitting in the back of the carriage.

"Wait a minute," Shank interrupted. "You trained the monkey to steal and give the articles to Quinn? You two are in cahoots with each other?"

"No," Dante shouted, trying to pull the animal off him with his cuffed hands. "I don't have anything to do with this little beast."

"Then explain why it's in your arms," Vaughn said.

While the argument continued, Lauralee stepped around her father and marched up the steps toward the five-and-dime store. From the front door, she pulled a small bell that announced customers. Walking to stand by the carriage, Lauralee let it peal.

Immediately, the monkey turned loose of Dante's neck and jumped into the carriage to sit next to Ophelia Istok. From its pocket it pulled a pair of earrings and laid them in the old woman's hands.

Shank walked toward the carriage. "You are in on it."

"They're not," Esme told the chief. "It's an old trick of my sister's. She curses a person with a stealing curse and then has Juka follow them around and place the articles near them."

"Juka?" the chief asked.

"The monkey. His name is Juka."

Shank faced Dante. "Did she curse you?"

"I was at a street party," Dante explained, looking as gloomy as he did when Shank first arrested him. "I recognized her, and she ran. I followed her, a couple of men beat me up, and then she cursed me."

Shank eyed him. "Can you prove it?"

"My friend Lamont took me to the doctor's afterward, and then things started missing out of the dorm rooms at Creighton University. The police thought I'd done it. I found jewelry on top of my desk afterward. I was too frightened to turn myself in. I left the pieces in the dorm and followed her, to try to get her to remove the curse."

"How did you recognize her?"

"She's my aunt, apparently. I thought she was my mother."

Shank took a step toward him. "You're Roma?"

Dante lifted his chin. "On my mother's side. I'm proud to be Roma."

"All right," Shank began. "I want you"—he pointed at Dante—"you, and you"—he pointed at Big Buck and Lauralee—"inside right now." He took another look at Esme. "If you don't mind, Mrs. Beckett, just for a moment, and then you can go with Todd and Oliver." After Esme nodded and stepped forward, Shank nodded to Casillo and Vaughn. "Bring this woman inside with the others."

The men moved toward Ophelia.

Lauralee followed, but before entering the building she found Felton Ewing on the front steps. "Well, what do you know about that, Mr. Ewing? I wasn't aiding a felon after all."

"We'll see about that. Nothing's been proven yet."

Axel Garvey laughed along with Billy Yank. "Ewing got it wrong again, didn't he? Half of writing his paper is hiding the truth from us."

Pastor Carmichael stood next to Wade Murphy and slapped him on the shoulder. "I never believed any of it, anyway."

Lauralee smiled into the paling face of Ewing. "How about an exclusive interview with me and the future governor of Colorado, Mr. Ewing?" She slipped both arms around her father's waist. "I'll explain what a good father he is and how he's influenced me to look for the good in a person."

A week later, and after Dante was cleared of all charges, except the one that spoke of Quinn causing Chief Shank to witness a half-naked woman rinsing her stockings, Lauralee sat in the parlor of Todd's house on the piano bench with Dante Quinn himself. He had come to formally call, but he'd stopped by to see Todd, and that's how he and Lauralee wound up in the parlor, speaking friendly like.

He played wonderfully, his strong and long fingers stroking the keys. They bumped shoulders now and again, and Lauralee thought she was in heaven. His dark hair was freshly washed and he'd shaved that morning. She could tell because his skin there was clear of stubble. Had he gussied up for her? Oh, how she wished that were true. Lauralee didn't know when she'd fallen in love with Dante Quinn exactly, but she had—hard.

She asked, "If your father died when you were ten, then who raised you?"

"I lived at the orphanage." He continued to play and looked at the keyboard instead of at her. "When I turned seventeen, I received my father's money. It was enough for me to go to the university."

"But . . . who loved you and cared for you?"

He glanced at her with a half smile and then down at the keyboard again. "I didn't want that. I wanted Emelina to find me." He looked so sad just then that she wanted to wrap him up and hold him. And if they kissed, that was all the better.

Instead, she asked, "Did you have friends?"

"One."

"One?"

"Yes. He was the most annoying kid at the home. No one else liked him. His name is Lamont Humphrey—which reminds me. I still need to return his car to him."

"That's not your car?"

He pretended offense. "That beat-up wreck behind Blue Bells? No." He continued to play lightly, beautifully.

Lauralee offered, "You play wonderfully."

"I knew I'd catch a woman one day if I played well enough." His dark eyes, bright and bold, looked into hers. "Do you play?"

She straightened with braggadocio. "I am enormously well bred, thank you." She placed her hands on the keys near his. "Enough of Bach. I'm in the mood for chopsticks."

They played well together and *loudly*. And when they'd struck the last chord, Dante turned on the seat and asked, "Will you come with me?"

Her heart soared. "Where?"

"I'd like to visit Wolf Whistle Creek."

Her heart dropped to the valley. She'd been hoping for something a *little bit* more romantic. But she said brightly, "I'd love to."

"Oh, there you are," Esme Beckett said, rushing to the fence of her garden and meeting Dante as he walked through the gate. "I've been watching out for you." In her gentle way, she took Dante's face into the palms of her hands. He had to bend toward her, and the feel of her rough hands touched something deep inside of him.

Happy tears rimmed her lashes. "I've lit a candle every day for you."

He saw the love his aunt had for him, and it took all Dante had within him not to break down himself. How could he have ever thought Ophelia looked like Emelina Quinn? This woman, Esme Beckett, Dante's aunt—she was what he remembered of his mother. Ophelia Istok, on the other hand, resembled what Dante's bitterness made Emelina out to be. "You are like her," he told Esme.

"In a small way, perhaps. Come," she said, dropping her hands. "Come inside." They walked arm in arm, he and Esme, and Esme with Lauralee too. The rounded door opened to a small front room, clean and smelling of the flowers that burst into bloom just outside the opened windows. There on the mantel was the candle Esme had spoken of; it was only an inch tall in its holder.

She served them tea with honey and biscuits that she'd made that morning. When Dante told her that Nolan Quinn died when he was but ten, she looked as if she would weep again. "If I had known, Dante, I would've searched for you. I would've brought you here to live. But your father never answered my letters. I thought perhaps he still lived."

"How long have you known that Emelina was dead?"

She set her cup on the small table beside her chair. "Ten years, perhaps. It was the last time I wrote to your father, to tell him how very sorry I was that she'd gone. He loved her to death."

"Yes, he did," Dante whispered, not explaining how Nolan Quinn died. "But by the time you'd written, he was gone too."

"I suppose so." She smiled sadly. "What have you heard about Ophelia? Oliver refuses to go to the police station and find out for me."

Dante could understand that. He wanted to forget Ophelia too. "Shank said she's to stand trial in a month for murder, or at least accessory to murder, for the death of Emelina Quinn." He set his cup aside too and pulled the stone from his shirt pocket and stared at it. "She still claims she should be judged by the Roma court."

Esme shook her head. "I don't understand that. They would be just as harsh, maybe more so, than the court in Victor City. She would be exiled, as Levi Bloodcrow was—"

"What?" Lauralee interrupted. "Levi was exiled?"

"Yes. That's why he lived out there at the abandoned camp. No gypsy camp would allow him to stay with them because he killed Emelina."

"For ten years?" Lauralee asked. "That's how long the queer lights have appeared."

"He was not always the way you saw him at the peak. He was once a handsome man, lean and strong. I loved him." She gazed out at the roses near the window. "We were betrothed when I discovered I was pregnant with Oliver. When my father found out, he sent me away. Levi never tried to find me. I met Matthew in Denver, and despite the fact that I was six months along, he loved me. He offered me a home when my own family disowned me.

"The next time I saw Levi, he'd changed. He'd spent too much time with Ophelia, I'm afraid, and with her black magic. He was harsh, angry. His hair was tangled, and he would never look me in the eye."

"Maybe he really did have a behavioral disorder," Lauralee said, quoting her Uncle Todd's medical tome. When both Dante and Esme gave her questioning looks, she shrugged. "Look how he turned out."

Esme glanced at Dante's hand. "What is the stone you have? Emelina wore one like it."

"She wore this one," he told her, holding the jewel in the sunbeam that played in the room. "The chief gave it to me when I told him that it belonged to my father's family."

"Is it a ruby?"

"No," Dante said. "He said it's a red emerald."

"I've never heard of a red emerald."

"I have no idea how much it's worth—"

"Oh," Lauralee cut in. "Is Mr. Petrova about? He's a jeweler. He can tell us about the stone."

Lauralee looked about the large front room of the Thompsons' old house. Someone had left books out. Shoes were scattered everywhere. The fireplace needed cleaning. And what an odd combination of odors; it smelled as if a trout had died but had eaten chocolate chip cookies before keeling over.

Obviously Mrs. Petrova was still ill.

Mr. Petrova, however, sat at the supper table with a gem glass stuck to his eye. He turned the stone over and over in his hands. He was short and balding, skinny too, which additionally pointed to the lady's bedridden state.

"Your father is correct, young man," Petrova told Dante. "A

ruby is a clearer red. This is indeed an emerald. Very rare. I've heard of its existence only recently, and as far as I know, the red emerald is found only here in the United States. Only in Utah, amazingly." He popped the eyepiece out and put it on the table. "I wish I could buy it from you."

"I'm not selling it," Dante told him. "I'll never do that. It's a family heirloom and very precious to me."

Petrova nodded and pushed out of the chair. "I understand. Do you know the red stone means many things to different people? To men, it indicates command, nobility, and vengeance. To a woman, it signifies her desire to take the command away from men."

"That's why Ophelia wanted the stone," Esme Beckett put in. She stood near the table next to Dante. "She wanted power and used the stone as an amulet."

"Yes, she did," Lauralee put in. "She told me so. She said she kept her spells and enchantments in it."

"But she will never have it again," Dante finished, putting the stone into his pocket. "Thank you, Mr. Petrova, for your assistance."

To Lauralee, it seemed there was determination in Dante again. It was as if he'd made a decision, and she didn't know what that decision was until they began their journey to Victor City.

"You're the first person I've trusted in so long. Now I'm going to trust you to understand something."

She waited for him to continue, but the beginning thread of the conversation scared her. He would tell her something she didn't want to hear . . . and then he said it: "I'm leaving in the morning."

Cold grabbed her heart. How could he leave? They were

meant to be together. The hurt of it came out with her voice. "Where are you going?"

"To return Lamont's car, first." He took a long breath. "I have to say good-bye to Emelina . . ."

"You have to leave to do that? You can't say good-bye to her here?" She held on to the seat of the day buggy. Rain fell in her heart and it started to drown her. Her lips hurt from the hard downward pull on them.

Dante said nothing. He didn't look at her but at the trail ahead of them. He snapped the reins lightly to keep the horse trotting.

She asked, "Will you come back?"

"I don't know. But don't wait for me, Lauralee. I know how hard waiting is, and I wouldn't wish that on anyone."

They rode in silence after that, and Lauralee knew the pain that Dante surely felt when his mother had left him; it was the agony that the separation from love caused. She wouldn't try to hold on to him. Dante knew what he wanted to do; somehow he needed it. She'd seen the resolve in his face and his jawline when he'd made his decision during their visit with Mr. Petrova.

Dante had put his trust in her. Lauralee would not smother it with a cry for him to stay. She would let him go and she would *trust* that if he loved her, he would return one day.

The difference between their sorrows was that Lauralee had others who loved her. Her father cherished her, her mother would never faint in her affection, and Rick, despite his condemnation of her gullibility, would die before he'd ever let anything happen to her. She could never doubt the strength of her family, no matter how stupidly she'd acted lately.

But it was the one for whom she'd acted stupidly that she wished loved her enough to stay. At least Dante had told her he was leaving. That was something he hadn't heard from his mother. Maybe that was what he wished to hear when he said his own farewells: her good-bye.

And Lauralee would be patient. She'd hold on to the love in her heart and cultivate it and not let it die or turn into bitterness. That was her decision, now and forever.

Chapter Twelve

The train whistle would have been enough of an announcement, but Oliver Beckett shouted above the noise, *"Train from Forge Rock arriving on time!"* Not a traveler stood on the platform. *"Next stop, Sterrrrling!"* If there were something she could count on, it was Oliver Beckett acting like the pompous banana that he was. That was what Lauralee thought while watching Beckett from her perch on the courthouse steps. It was autumn now, October, in fact, and the leaves had already begun to turn yellow and russet under the sun. A cool breeze came off the mountains, swept along the west road, and blew the courthouse flag above her head.

Dante had been gone seventy-two days.

Piper interrupted her musings. "Efren and I are going to Wolf Whistle Creek this evening for the harvest celebration. Do you want to come along? We're going to get our palms read."

A twinge stuck her in the abdomen and she shook her head. "No thanks—"

"Lauralee." Piper cut her off. "You need to start getting out." Her green eyes looked more like jewels with the autumn

180

sky behind her. Strawberry blond hair fell in waves around her pretty face—pretty but very contrary at the moment. "All you do anymore is sit at home."

"I come out all the time."

She threw up her hands. "To sit out here and watch the train. Are you expecting Dante to step off it someday?"

"No," she lied. "Dante's gone."

Piper slipped down to sit on the step beside her, and she put her arm around Lauralee's shoulders. "You're accepting it. Good. But you need to get out, and I insist you come with us tonight."

Lauralee groaned.

"I mean it. You must come." She stood again, ready to leave. "We'll pick you up after supper and take you in our carriage. And don't give me that face. You're coming. Efren is already expecting to drive us there in his carriage."

Lauralee got to her feet as well. "What do you see in Efren Vaughn?"

"I like him. He's very sweet. You two never hit it off, I know, but I'm through playing hard to get with Rick Murphy."

Lauralee laughed at her. "I'm sure he could never tell that you liked him."

"Well, that's over now, anyway . . . So I've got to go. I'll see you this evening." She turned, ready to take the steps, but saw who climbed them just below her. Piper spun around with a horrible look of panic on her face. "Do you think he heard me?"

"No," Lauralee told her and then smiled at her brother. "Hello, Rick. What do you know?"

"That you're loafing as usual." He glanced at Piper. "Hello, Piper."

"Hello," she said shortly, and then, "I'm off to meet my favorite deputy for lunch. Good-bye, you two."

And then she was gone, and Lauralee was left to stand next

to Rick, who watched Piper descend the steps. "Does she ever mention me?" he asked.

"Who?"

"Piper. Does she ever say I'm attractive or . . . you know, anything like that?"

She teetered . . . and then laughed harder. "You're kidding, right?"

His straight mouth turned down at the corners, and he narrowed his pale blue eyes.

Lauralee cleared her throat. "No, she's never mentioned anything like that."

He took her elbow and they walked down the steps together. "Do you think she really likes Efren Vaughn, or is she just stepping out with him because no one else has asked?"

"Why are you asking me these things?" she said, thinking her brother was confident enough to ask any woman out whom he wanted to; he never questioned himself at all regarding friendships.

"Because I trust your judgment, Lauralee. As it turns out, you're a fairly good judge of character."

Rick continued. "If you say Piper's happy, then I'll believe she's happy."

Lauralee thought about that for a moment. "I think she's happy," she told him, nodding to herself, and knowing that it was the correct answer to give. If Rick thought Piper wasn't serious about Vaughn, then he would act too slowly about stepping in. As it was, she knew her brother. He liked a challenge.

Lauralee would be glad when her parents returned from Denver. They were spending more time there, since the elections would be held next month. It was the reason she was staying with Uncle Todd again. In the spare room she dressed in her gray skirt and white blouse. Pulling her hair into a French twist, she stepped onto the landing when Piper knocked on the front door.

"I don't want to stay long," Lauralee told her, meeting her at the bottom of the steps.

"We'll leave any time you want to," Piper promised. "But I must have another card reading. You know I took the advice last time that the woman Roza gave me. I considered something that I never did before: Efren!"

That was Lauralee's reminder to *not* take a gypsy's advice.

They rode southwestward just as the sun went down beneath the Rocky Mountains range. The lamps of Wolf Whistle Creek, far off, twinkled in the valley. The cool evening came, and the early-night wind whispered in the leaves along the way.

Finally, the Wolf Creek flowed slow and broad on their left. The water gleamed pale in the moonlight, and the sound of a violin pierced the night. Laughter leaped to the sky. Silver lanterns hung from the pawpaw trees, showing the gypsies all around the camp. There were many other folks too: those from Wolf Whistle Creek, Victor City, and some from Sterling as well. In the middle of the wagons was a ring of stone seats to behold the fire built to stave off the coolness in the air. She knew this place well. Though she'd come here only twice, she'd seen it many times in her mind. It was then that she realized her mother had been correct. The most romantic times in her life had been when she'd fought and argued with Dante Quinn.

Lauralee walked with Piper and Efren as they strolled hand in hand. He bought them both sweet cakes, and Lauralee picked at the food, not hungry at all. Then she saw the man Casamir. He stood inside the horse corral, handling a black stallion that had been harnessed and broken. Speaking to the crowd, he said, "This is a horse worthy of a gypsy. He ran these ranges for many years but now is tamed to do our bidding with love and honor . . ."

She smiled at that and moved along when Efren and Piper did. And then Lauralee saw her: Roza. In the lamplight she was more beautiful than any woman Lauralee had ever seen. Raven, dark, enchanting she was, and she sat at a table showing cards to a woman. Large golden hoops dangled from her ears. Her bracelets tinkled with her every movement.

"I'm staying right here until I get my palm read," Piper told Efren and Lauralee. She joined the line waiting to see Roza. Efren rolled his eyes and followed her, but Lauralee wandered to the next wagon. Would Dante wind up here one day? Perhaps he would. He'd drunk the love potion . . .

"T'aves mansa," someone said inside the nearby wagon. There were tiny candles lighting the inside of it, and the woman who spoke to her had many veils over her head. She repeated, *"T'aves mansa."*

"I don't understand," Lauralee told her, feeling a bit fearful of the woman and her mysterious manner.

"Come with me."

"Where?"

"Inside, *t'aves* . . ."

"Er, no thank you," she told her, stepping backward. "I'm getting ready to leave."

The gypsy woman moved to the edge of the wagon and held out her hand. "Not yet. I must see your palm. You have *kpashe, va?"*

Was it Ophelia Istok? No, it couldn't be; she'd been sentenced to the penitentiary in Denver. Besides, this woman was larger than Ophelia. Lauralee couldn't make out her features beneath the veils, but she would guess this woman to be younger than the old gypsy woman. Her voice sounded lower too. Possibly because she whispered rather than spoke out. "I will not harm you, *Chav*. I know of you."

"How do you know me?"

"He told me of your beauty, your love. He told me this."

"Who is my love?" she asked, stepping forward now.

"I will tell you if you let me see your palm."

Lauralee shook her head. "I didn't bring money—"

"I don't want your money."

She hesitated only a moment more, and then Lauralee held out her hand. The gypsy said, "You have thick hands."

"I know—"

Suddenly, the gypsy placed something in her hand. Lauralee leaned forward to see the red-stoned ring, and she demanded, "Where did you get this!"

Dante pulled the veils off his head and grinned at her. "Oh," he said in a happy voice. "It was my father's. It's a family heirloom."

"Dante Quinn!" she demanded stupidly, pulling her hand roughly from his. "What are you doing here?"

He made a grab for her wrist. "Don't lose the ring."

"What?" She opened her palm. It still was in her grasp, and she saw that the stone indeed was gold-lined now and made into a lady's ring.

"Oh, thank goodness," he said, hopping out of the wagon. "You gave me a scare. That is very precious to me."

She gazed at him and into his dark, dark eyes. He was more beautiful than she ever remembered him. Maybe it was because he smiled. The lamplights gleamed upon him and he was golden and perfect and healthy and whole. She held out her hand to return the ring to him.

He closed her fingers over it again. "It is for you. You are more precious to me than even the stone. I want you to wear it." His arm went around her waist and he pulled her close to him. "Do you know that I love you?"

She grinned through her tears, and she nodded because she was afraid to speak. Words would surely choke her.

"Er . . . do you love me back? I was hoping you'd say that you do."

Lauralee laughed and nodded her head. "Yes, I do."

"Good." He took the ring and slid it onto her finger. "You are mine."

She threw her arms around his neck and pulled him to her in a tight embrace. When she turned loose, just a smidgen, his hands found her face and he kissed her firmly. When he at last released her, she asked, "Where did you go?"

"San Francisco. I stood by the bay. The water is the color of your eyes, by the way." He kissed her again and then continued. "I told my mother that I loved her and that I was sorry that I'd been angry for so long. And I said good-bye."

Lauralee nodded. "And you will stay here now?"

"Well, you're here, and my job is here—"

"What job?" she asked, pulling away from him.

He kept his hands on her waist. "I'll be assisting Judge Mitchell until he decides to retire from the courts."

"Judge Mitchell? He never said a word."

"Well, I hope not," Dante told her. "I was trusting him to keep quiet. Just as I trusted your friends to get you here to-night." He nodded and spun her round to see Piper and Efren standing a few feet away. They stood there linked arm in arm and grinning madly.

Lauralee laughed at them and then turned to Dante again. "I'm so glad you've come back."

"I had to come back, if for nothing more than for the love of Lauralee."